£6.99

Sisters

Emily Sutherland

OPENBOOK
PUBLISHERS

Published edition copyright © Openbook Publishers 1994
Text copyright © Emily Sutherland 1994
Cover design by Graeme Cogdell
Cover illustration by Robert Roennfeldt

First printing February 1994
01 00 99 98 97 96 95 94   9 8 7 6 5 4 3 2 1

National Library of Australia
Cataloguing-in-Publication entry

Sutherland, Emily.
  Sisters.

  ISBN 0 85910 635 7.

  I. Title.

A823.3

Typeset by Openbook Publishers in 10pt Clearface Regular

Printed and published by
Openbook Publishers
205 Halifax Street
Adelaide, South Australia   1544-93

Chapter One

The smell of floor wax always reminded Eileen of cleaning the old convent every Saturday.

Sister Celine would place a small vase of flowers at the foot of the statue of Our Lady of Lourdes in the chapel. If the sun shone through the window it shrouded Our Lady and the flowers in a soft purple and gold tint. Royal colours for the Queen of Heaven, Sister Celine would say.

Most of the older nuns were dead now. Gone to their eternal rest and probably polishing everything in heaven. They could cope more easily with concupiscence than clutter.

The old convent had been built over a hundred years ago on a hill overlooking the city, detached and sheltered. Then it had been surrounded by bushland, the driveway leading down to the road by the river. Today it was surrounded by houses whose owners had certainly not taken a vow of poverty.

In line with changing needs the building was no longer the novitiate but a seminar centre. People met there to talk, grow, and discover, sheltered by the cloisters which stood as a reminder of a more-ordered spiritual regime. Those early nuns had planted trees and established secluded corners where flowers bloomed. There was still an air of tranquillity despite the comings and goings of those seeking renewal.

Eileen, coming down from her headstand, swung her feet to the floor, keeping her head down while she counted to one hundred, allowing the blood flow to equalise, then sat up. Still sitting on the floor she reached across for her New Testament. Some mornings she chose the particular reading for the day. Other times she opened it at random, thinking to find some mystic guidance. Today was a random day.

'You know me, and you know whence I come; but I have not come on my own errand, I was sent by one who has a right to send; and him you do not know.'

Fitting words for a parish worker. Eileen closed her eyes, withdrawing into herself.

She stood at the edge of the crowd. The temple was cool, although she was aware of the heat, dust, and noise outside. Men jostled, sceptics rubbed shoulders with believers, trying to hear the words of the preacher. She felt rather than understood.

'Dear Lord, let me be your messenger. I do not ask for miracles, only life in abundance.'

Twenty minutes yoga and half an hour meditation. You couldn't get more ecumenical than that. Would Sister Celine have accepted the yoga? With no more ease than she would have accepted the bare-limbed women who wandered around her beloved garden. Or the bare-headed nuns who instructed them.

Mary weeps when she sees a young lady with bare arms, Sister Josephine had told them.

I don't believe that, she had wanted to say but didn't dare. No one contradicted Sister Josephine.

Marion, always top of the Christian doctrine class, was the one they thought would become a nun. She made lots of visits to the chapel at lunchtime, splashing about with the holy water and making huge signs of the cross. Eileen didn't even consider the idea until she made her second retreat, at the age of fifteen. She stayed at school for two days of silence, listening to spiritual talks, reading holy books, and thinking holy thoughts. What holier thought than becoming a nun?

Back home she reverted to her former ambition to become an actress or an art teacher.

She considered the nun business again when she turned seventeen. The idea disturbed rather than attracted. She dismissed the idea. Her matric exams took all her attention. The day she went to buy her university textbooks she told her family. Books were off the shopping list, replaced by white nighties and sensible shoes. She knew she was being worldly but she hated the shoes.

Her younger sister, Clare, only thirteen months her junior, and her closest companion, cried every night for a week before she entered. Her older brother, Gregory, said they were wasted tears. He knew the nuns were hard up for recruits but they couldn't be that desperate. They would send Eileen home within a fortnight. Part of her hoped that he was right. God couldn't reproach her then, and she could go to university with her friends.

The other part of her felt sure that God had called her in a special way to serve him. The handmaiden of the Lord. It was a wonder that they had accepted her with ideas like that. Silly romantic piety. No place for it in the reality of convent life. Can steel be forged from marshmallow?

Occasionally Eileen returned to the old convent, where she had served her novitiate, to help conduct seminars. Once she had been asked to give a talk entitled: The Role of Women in the Church throughout History. The temptation had been to say simply: 'A very minor, underrated, and demeaning one', then sit down. Instead, she expanded the idea that the church was a human institution which reflected society rather than seeking to mould and change it. The role of women within the church didn't differ greatly from that of women in society generally. In other words, when the plum jobs were handed out they went to the men. Today women still had to assert themselves to change the system. If they didn't like it, work to alter it. Equality does not cease at the church door.

The women at the seminar didn't quite draw up a manifesto or leap to their feet and sing 'We shall overcome', but they did move to establish a committee to study female liberation theology and advise the bishop on ways to increase the role of women in the administration of the diocese. When it dawned on him that they meant more than extra help with the typing, he thanked them frostily, acknowledged their enthusiasm, however misguided, reminded them that most parishes had an altar society and disbanded the committee. Eileen wasn't asked to address a seminar for a long time after that.

No good unleashing us from our convents and then trying to muzzle us, she thought.

The house they now lived in differed from the others in the street only in the cross erected on the front verandah. Gothic ceilings and antique furniture do not a community make, and Eileen, Pauline, and Anne, the survivors from that early old convent, still lived their vows and religious calling in the confines of a three-bedroom brick-veneer dwelling. Even Sister Celine agreed that they were more effective in the world if they weren't locked up every night at six-thirty. Pauline said she could do with a bit more locking up and a bit less going to meetings every night, to which Anne would reply that the only way to stop Pauline from perpetual motion was to lock her up and tie her to the bedpost. Eileen thought of the headline: **Nuns in bondage**, but said nothing. Anne had a very prudish streak.

'Do you realise that none of the great religions of the world were founded by women?'

Pauline looked up from the newspaper and finished chewing her toast before replying. 'So? Thinking of starting one? Here, happy birthday.' She handed Eileen a large packet of herbal tea decorated with a red ribbon and a hand-painted card.

Pauline watched her as she read the card. 'You don't look any older. Must be your round, cheerful face. Keeps the wrinkles at bay.'

Eileen had forgotten it was her birthday. When she was little, birthdays had been days of great rejoicing, presents at the end of the bed waiting for her to wake up, favourite meals, being Daddy's 'little princess'.

In the convent they hadn't really worried about birthdays. Saints feast days were more important. Since she had turned forty, Eileen hadn't kept close watch on her age. Not through vanity — nuns don't have to fear growing old — but because she had other things to think about.

'You took your final vows over twenty years ago', Pauline was saying. 'And that was two days before your birthday. I remember Sister Celine gave you a rose from her garden and you put it in a vase near the statue of St Joseph. I thought that was funny, because he is the patron of happy marriages. Strange the things that stay in your memory. Anyway, happy birthday. Don't forget it's your turn to cook tonight and we are nearly out of potatoes. See you tonight. I've got three free periods and two reliefs today. You can't win!'

She picked up a basket filled with schoolbooks, a bread roll, an apple, and a pair of running shoes. Must be cross-country team training after school, Eileen thought. She wished she had half Pauline's energy.

Eileen was the parish worker. A mopper-upper she called herself. Mop up tears, mop up messes, try to mop up loneliness and hurting. Sister Celine's flowers were no longer adequate; they symbolised another era.

When she had told her family about her desire to become a nun they had made little comment. To her surprise her mother didn't seem surprised. She helped her prepare her trousseau, as it was quaintly called. On the day she was to enter, her mother drove her to the convent. Her father gave her a long hug and wished her 'God bless' at the front door. She hoped she was doing the right thing. Her mother started to cry as she drove. 'A wonderful life . . . God's will, I'm sure . . . your aunty wanted to be a nun, you know . . . oh, I'll miss you, dear.'

Eileen looked out of the car window at the tree-lined streets. Summer flowers were just beginning to fade. Colourfully dressed people strolled in the early-afternoon sunshine. She noticed an old lady being led by a small terrier. The scene became blurred as she looked through tear-filled eyes, and she reached over and touched her mother on the arm. It was then she knew that she had made a terrible mistake. She wasn't meant for the convent. She should be at the beach with her friends. What a fanciful idea, God wanting her to be a nun. She could think about it again when she had finished university.

'A vocation is a special call from God. It is the greatest gift he can give you.' Sister Josephine's face took on a kind of pinched ecstasy.

'Many are called but few are chosen. Of course you all have a vocation. God has a plan for each one of you. But some are called in a particular way to serve him in the religious life. If you are thus called and you deny him you will never really be happy. One of the girls I was at school with had a vocation, and she wanted to enter at the same time I did.' Sister Josephine paused, sure of her audience. 'Her parents were quite rich. They did all in their power to distract her and finally she lost her vocation and married a young man. He wasn't a Catholic either.'

Another pause. 'My friend didn't know a moment's happiness from her wedding day. I still pray for her. Remember the rich man who turned away from Jesus? Do you think he was ever happy again? I doubt it. God has given us everything . . . everything. He cannot be outdone in generosity.'

Sister Josephine had beautiful brown eyes. Five girls in the class decided to be nuns. Eileen wasn't one of them.

She should have trusted her earlier judgment. Eileen drew in her breath, about to ask her mother to turn the car around and go back home just as they entered the convent driveway through the big iron gates. She saw the high stone facade, the ornate wrought-iron balcony, and the small upstairs windows. Reverend Mother and the novice mistress, Mother Eleanor, were standing at the front door, smiling in welcome. Both seemed happy she was there. Reverend Mother greeted her with an embrace which managed to be disembodied and warm at the same time. Eileen decided to tell them about the mistake later, after she had prayed in the chapel. Then it would seem like divine intervention and be less embarrassing.

Reverend Mother invited them into the convent parlour. Eileen's mother blinked when she saw the antique furniture, and wondered if the nuns had any idea that they were sitting, literally, on a fortune. Eileen noticed the smell of wax.

Every time she wanted to lean back against the stall she noted the row of straight backs in front of her. The recitation of the office soothed her. She jerked her head up with a start. Going to sleep in chapel didn't quite bring excommunication, but almost.

Bells summoned and sent. Nuns were busy all day. Only at evening recreation did they sit and relax. Even then it was with knitting or sewing. The more gifted embroidered exquisite vestments. Eileen was knitting a pair of fingerless black gloves.

Sister Josephine had worn a pair in winter even in the classroom. The school was high-ceilinged and cold. The few lucky ones who sat near the small, warm fire worked in smug comfort. The rest of them felt chilly, and offered it up for the souls in purgatory. Sister Josephine told them it was best not to think about themselves or their comfort too much. If they forgot they were cold they would feel warm. She told them the same thing in summer, only in reverse. Despite her white coif and voluminous clothes she seemed to stay cool. In winter her only concession was her fingerless gloves.

Morning mass. A fresh start. She tried hard to pray it well and offer up her thoughts and actions of the day for the intentions of all the sisters. She prayed that she would be a good nun. She prayed that she wouldn't think uncharitable thoughts about Anne, the other postulant, but, dear Lord, she would try the patience of a saint. So immature, giggling at everything, and she didn't seem to have much to say when they were discussing the meditations and readings. She stopped her thoughts. Had she been uncharitable? Had she allowed her thoughts to continue when she realised she was being uncharitable? Dear God, please help me to be more tolerant. Mary, teach me humility.

Mother Eleanor said that true humility came from knowing ourselves for what we were, miserable sinners. Eileen tried, but she couldn't think of herself as a miserable sinner or the most unworthy creature before God. After all, she had entered the convent straight from school. That hadn't given her much chance to be a sinner.

Mother Eleanor said that if she had been protected from the evil excesses of the world then that was due to God's mercy. She should remember that much is expected from those to whom much has been given.

Anne told her later, in the strictest confidence, that she had let a boy kiss her at a party. She wondered if that had been a mortal sin, because she was almost sure then that she was going to be a nun. It wasn't a really long one, she had added. Eileen felt the problem theologically beyond her.

Sister Josephine had strict ideas about how they were to conduct themselves. The ideal was to be ladylike and modest, never drawing attention to themselves. Mary was their model, especially in obedience and holy purity. No boy would respect them if they sinned, even slightly, against holy purity. Boys might like to have a good time with you if you behaved in an immodest manner, but it was the good girl, the pure girl, who had respect for her body as the temple of the Holy Ghost, whom they would later marry. Sister Josephine told them of Amy who had gone to a dance and refused to go outside with a young man. 'I have come to dance, and dance I will', she had asserted. 'That young man was impressed by Amy's attitude. She had gained his respect, and that respect grew to love, and later they were married.'

On Thursday afternoons they had needlework, which consisted of the girls doing embroidery or knitting while Sister Josephine read to them. They loved these afternoons. When in a good mood, Sister read from Enid Blyton, although she would stop from time to time, frowning slightly, and ask them if they were sure that they wanted to hear about the Famous Five, especially George, who was no example to any of them. Other times she would choose something more edifying. *Daughters of the United Kingdom* was one of her favourites. It told of three girls in a boarding school, one from England, one from Scotland, and one Irish, who were paragons of virtue and piety. She wept at the sad parts, blowing her nose and saying: 'You girls must have hearts of stone'. In extremis she would read from a book on etiquette which had detailed instructions about when to shake hands, when to wear gloves, what to do if you met the king and queen, and not to spit in the spitoon. Sister would chant epigrams of excellence. 'Punctuality is the courtesy of kings; let us all be little queens', then smile at them over her spectacles. For her the path to righteousness might be thorny, but it was clearly signposted.

Going to a Catholic school had prepared her a little for life in the convent, but Eileen still found it very different from home. Everything in the big old building was cold. The other postulants were friendly, but they were discouraged from making special friends. Their cells were cold. The water they had placed in the dish the night before was freezing by the time they came to wash in the morning. She missed coming home to her family each evening, her mother listening to the tales of her doings while she rolled pastry, or prepared a stew, laughing at the funny bits. She even missed her quarrels with Clare over who had borrowed which jumper from whom and left it in a heap on the bedroom floor. And her brother's teasing. Christian charity did not compensate for family support and love.

Chapter Two

High vaulted ceilings supported by stained wooden beams. Sanctuary lamp flickering red. Rows of black straight backs. Clear voices giving the responses.

Introibo ad altare Dei.
Ad Deum qui laetificat juventutem meam.

No nun was allowed in the sanctuary during mass, because she was a woman, but on the frequent occasions when the altar boy did not arrive for early mass, Sister Rosaria knelt at the altar rails and rang the small tri-domed bell at the solemn parts. Once to warn, six times at the consecration, and again at the *Domine, non sum dignus* (Lord, I am not worthy). A ritual stretching back through centuries. Later Eileen was to think of the Latin mass in terms of archetypal memory. The familiar if meaningless words (for how many of the congregation understood Latin?) being recited in churches throughout the world. She followed in English from her missal. Had she lived in France she would have followed in French. The same mass, the same ceremony, the same doctrine which they all believed. The rock which was Peter and all the popes in an unbroken sequence. As it was and would be world without end.

In summer the altar was lit by the morning sun, the brass candlesticks and crucifix gleaming. During winter mornings they needed the lights, which gave a cosier glow. On special feast days the nuns sang a hymn after mass. They rarely sang during the ceremony, and not in that most solemn time after communion when they had received the body of our Lord. That was their time. She had to learn to hold the large rosary beads against her thigh to prevent them rattling, as she took her place in the choir or left her stall to approach the altar rails and receive communion. She learnt to raise the wooden seat without noise. She learnt to turn the pages of her missal soundlessly. She walked with her eyes downcast; custody of the eyes encouraged custody of the thoughts. Her prayers were undisciplined, sometimes reveries. Mother Eleanor cautioned her. Were her distractions deliberately sought? She should have more structure to her prayer. There were many excellent books which would help her. Eileen tried, but often found her thoughts wandering to home and her family. She wondered if God would mind. Was Jesus ever homesick?

They were to be Marthas rather than Marys. Lots of cleaning, a turn at the cooking and gardening. The gardening she didn't mind in the least. Out of doors, digging in soil, and seeing the result of her efforts blazing in colour. The postulants and novices didn't mix with the professed nuns. They were in training and would be either a distraction or distracted. She was never sure which. Mother Eleanor guided her and Anne and the other novices until the day they were to take their vows. Two years novitiate seemed a long time, especially when a lot of it was spent learning how to polish a wooden floor until it gleamed. She who is faithful in little things can be trusted with much, reminded Mother Eleanor. Did dust behind the piano really mean a lower place in heaven?

Clare came to see her quite often. She was now at university studying Arts ('Doesn't everyone? It's such a wonderfully useless qualification') and ensuring that her social life was 'fantastic'.

Eileen wondered if Clare was becoming brittle and superficial. She noticed her starting to swear a lot, then looking around the parlour and giggling at the thought that she had shocked all the ghosts of the dead nuns. More likely to shock Sister Josephine, who might be walking past and who had very acute hearing. Eileen's mother worried about Clare, although she continued to attend Sunday mass and even benediction some Sunday evenings. She asked Eileen to pray for Clare when Clare started seeing a lot of Alan. 'A charming enough young man, I grant you, but an atheist. Very sure of himself. I don't really think he and Clare are meant for each other.'

Her father labelled him an arrogant young know-all.

Clare thought he was wonderful and talked about him more and more each time she visited. By the time she was in her final year she was talking of plans to become engaged, openly questioning her religion, and hinting that virginity was not necessarily the highest state.

Their mother redoubled her prayers and said nothing. She hoped that Clare's good sense would prevail before she did anything foolish. Eileen was the only person to whom she could confide her fears fully.

The novitiate is a testing time. Mother Eleanor was not fully convinced of Eileen's progress. She wasn't happy with the way she strode down the corridor. 'Strive for an inconspicuous demeanour. Cultivate forgetfulness of self and true humility. From humility grows love, and the love of God is the most important thing for us all. You don't have to think you are incompetent or worthless. God sent his only Son to redeem you. Surely that means you are worth something in his eyes. But see yourself in relation to God and strive to do his holy will at all times. Don't be concerned with Eileen's will. Be faithful in little things, like St Thérèse, the Little Flower.'

Eileen read St Thérèse's autobiography and found it irritating. Thérèse seemed to have limited interests. She preferred the other St Teresa who stormed about Spain telling the Carmelite order that it had gone off the rails and needed to pull its socks up and return to the original spirit of Carmel. Eileen wondered if she should have chosen an enclosed order. It must be easier to be holy when you remove yourself completely from the world. Or a missionary. You would feel that you were getting somewhere living in primitive surroundings and preaching God's word to pagans. Imagine the joy when one was baptised! Being faithful in little things was much harder, because nobody noticed except when you failed.

It was different for Anne. She was used to not drawing attention to herself. Eileen was energetic, boisterous even. Her laugh was distinctive. Nuns are meant to be cheerful but not loud.

Anne never had any visitors. She hinted that her family lived in another state. She never received any letters either. Eileen found that strange. She had never known anything but a warm, loving family, but Anne seemed not to care. Perhaps she is further along the path of holiness than I am, thought Eileen, and has achieved true detachment from worldly things. Later Anne told her that she didn't even know if her parents were alive. She had been deserted by her mother when she was three and brought up by a very stern grandmother who was now dead. 'The Sisters are the first family I have ever known', she said. 'I love being here, because I feel I belong, and all the nuns are so kind. I think of you as my sister in a special way, because we entered together.' Eileen came closer to understanding humility.

She used to think that the day she was professed would be the culmination of all her desires, an acceptance by God of the sacrifice of her life, and she would live forevermore in a glow of self-approval. That was long before Mother Eleanor got at her. Now she saw her profession as the beginning of a long climb towards the peak of the mountain. At the peak was spiritual perfection, and the only sure thing about it was that you never reached it. The nearer you got the less perfect you perceived yourself. At times you came closer to understanding the true nature of God and his love for his people. In a personal way you grew closer. It wasn't just abstract understanding.

They all wore long white dresses, like brides. They were the brides of Christ. Eileen's mother bought her a classic, simple dress, obviously with Clare in mind as well. Eileen wore her mother's bridal veil and carried a small posy of tiny roses.

Now she was sure. Her heart was full of love for God. However, for weeks before, she had been tormented by doubts. Was she doing the right thing? Was it just pride that made her feel she had been chosen by God? Was it just an insurance policy to get into heaven? Couldn't she serve God as well and more comfortably in the world? She felt lonely. There was no-one she could really talk to except Mother Eleanor, who was a wise, old, detached lady. She understood what you said, but she didn't touch you. There was little opportunity to talk to the other novices. They maintained silence during the day, unless it was strictly necessary to speak, and at recreation they sat in a group, knitting, sewing, or embroidering. Idle gossip was forbidden and heart-to-hearts completely taboo. Eileen realised that you could live for years in the convent and never utter a word, and nobody need realise. There was love and caring but no real contact. Personal friendships were against the spirit of the order. Mother Eleanor loved to quote from *The Imitation of Christ*:

> Never desire to be singularly praised or loved; for this belongs to God alone, who has none like to himself.
>
> Neither desire that any one's heart should be taken up with you; nor you be much taken up with the love of any one; but let Jesus be in you, and in every good man.
>
> Be pure and free inwardly, and be not entangled by any creature.

In later years she heard that convents were notorious hotbeds of lesbianism, and laughed. 'All latent in our case. We were repressed, possibly, but too busy and organised to be concerned with our sexuality. That came later.'

It was decreed that Eileen, now Sister Mary Patrice, and Anne, now Sister Mary Catherine, were to attend the university and study Arts in order to qualify as teachers. Mother Eleanor supported the idea of study but vetoed philosophy as potentially dangerous to one's faith. All the truths one needed to know were to be found in the teachings of the church and holy Scripture, and even there one needed guidance. The devil set up many snares for unwary creatures, and all the knowledge in the world could not compensate for the loss of one's immortal soul.

Eileen felt the stirrings of the rebellious feelings she thought she had subdued forever. How could the pursuit of truth lead her away from God? What about St Thomas Aquinas?

'Ah, he was a man, and a brilliant one at that.'

Reverend Mother preferred them to enrol for the same subjects so they could travel together and attend the same lectures. They settled in to an undergraduate routine.

University cloisters buzzed with life and argument, unlike the cloisters at the convent. A fashionable atheism was prevalent, never threatened by the colourless Evangelical Union students, who preyed upon unwary coffee drinkers. There were more questions than solutions. It's a pity they don't all realise that Reverend Mother has the answers, and what she doesn't know you can find out from the provincial, the bishop, or, as a last resort, the pope, thought Eileen. She and Anne ate sandwiches in a secluded corner of the Union cafeteria, having been given special permission to eat in public. Stephen had told them the famous joke about the caf coffee being sent to an institution for analysis and the report coming back: Your camel has diabetes.

He was hoping to shock, but Stephen's jokes they could handle. What Eileen did find difficult was the history tutor holding her personally responsible for the excesses of the Spanish Inquisition. She was prepared to admit that it wasn't the church's finest hour, but didn't see the necessity to do so every week. They attended the annual debate: 'Does God exist?' feeling conspicuous in their habits and embarrassed because the speaker for the negative was the more convincing. Anne added the atheist speaker, who was very handsome, to her prayer list.

Examinations. Success. Was she sinning against pride to feel pleased that she had done well? Not when she realised that Anne had done even better. Who would have thought her a scholar? They both finished their first degree, and then Anne began her Masters, studying at night and teaching during the day. Eileen left the academic honours for others, and coached the school tennis team.

Chapter Three

Karen's house always managed to look untidy. Eileen thought, you could hardly expect her to prune her rosebush when she didn't bother to pick up all the debris on the verandah. Karen had been on her hospital visiting list, and even then she had noted that her bed and hospital cubicle looked untidy, although the baby had been neatly folded into his bassinet. One sensed the hand of a nurse.

Karen's card had said she was a Catholic but failed to mention that she hadn't been near a church for years. Eileen didn't hold that against her. Karen was also an orphan and a deserted woman, never having been a wife. Eileen didn't hold that against her either. We are all entitled to a certain amount of bad management. Karen, having recognised a saviour in Eileen, was to be with her for some time to come. The very inertia which made her irritating ensured continued support.

The new baby had a red, squashed, cabbage face. Amber-Mae, his sister, hovered near the bassinet. Karen was still in bed, smoking. Eileen moved the bassinet away from the stream of smoke.

'He's a little devil. Cried half the night. Gawd, I'm tired', announced Karen.

Amber-Mae came closer and took Eileen's hand.

'Get out of that Amber-Mae. Sister doesn't want you clinging. Go and play.'

Amber-Mae's grip did not relax. Eileen led her over to the bassinet and asked her where the powder and facecloth were kept. It was obvious that little Aaron needed a new nappy.

The house looked a little tidier when she left. Amber-Mae looked cleaner. Karen had had a little weep over the disappearance of Aaron's father, who hadn't been sighted for several months. Eileen felt a sense of frustration. What do you say to a young woman who has two children by two different men, neither of whom stayed around for the birth of his child? How can you help a young woman who seems programmed for failure? What chance did the children really have? What could she do apart from clean up a little, tell Amber-Mae a story about when Jesus was a baby, and collect the junk mail from the verandah as she left? A mess only partially mopped up.

Chapter Four

Sister Josephine had been a staunch royalist although pained by a photo of the queen wearing slacks. She encouraged them to pray for the conversion of Elizabeth back to the faith of her fathers, unaware of the constitutional havoc it would have caused had their prayers been answered.

They were warned against mixed marriages. Men made promises not always kept. Sister Josephine knew of a girl who had married a man who had no religion at all. 'Imagine that, girls. He never knew the love of God or the guidance of Holy Mother Church!'

This man had promised his bride that he would never interfere in her religious devotions and would allow her to bring up their children as Catholics. But, as she genuflected towards the blessed sacrament after the wedding ceremony she heard him mutter: 'That's the last time you'll do that, my dear'. That girl left her husband straightaway and went back to live with her parents.

Uncle Gerard had married Aunt Thelma outside the church. His father never spoke to him again. Eileen's mother had a soft spot for Thelma, because she had never heard her say an uncharitable word about anyone, and that is rare in Catholic or Protestant. Eileen prayed for them both every Christmas.

'Mind if I turn on the television? There's a program on bio-ethics I need to watch.'

Anne settled in the comfortable chair. The volume was too loud. She put on her reading glasses and started to take notes, peering over the top when she wanted to focus on the screen.

Where were bio-ethics when Karen was conceiving? thought Eileen. There seemed to be too large a gap between the theologians and life as she encountered it.

Pauline was washing up. 'Eileen, did you cook rice because you thought it would go with the chicken, or because you forgot to buy potatoes?'

'Yes.'

'The meat was a bit tough', said Anne.

Mother Eleanor had told them it was just as bad being picky and delicate about their food as it was to be greedy.

'I suspect it was old chook masquerading as spring chicken. Would you like some birthday cake with your coffee?'

Anne was working hard on her thesis and was often tense. Eileen offered to teach her yoga, but she said she didn't have the time to tie herself into a knot. Pauline suggested a walk before dinner each evening. Anne said she'd love to but she didn't have the energy.

'Shared-lunch tomorrow. End-of-year staff do. What can I take this time?' called Pauline from the kitchen.

'Can't you go empty-handed and look surprised? There's always too much to eat at those lunches.'

'Eileen! I can see you've been away from teaching too long. I'll make a pineapple cheesecake.'

Pauline sang softly as she cooked. Eileen wrote a letter to her brother until the television program was finished. Then the three women knelt down, closed their eyes, and began their evening prayer. It was Anne's turn to lead the prayer.

'O God, we thank you for this day and all the blessings that you have given us. Help us to bring your love and peace to all those we encounter. Guide us in the paths of righteousness. Bless our endeavours. Bring comfort to the sorrowing, justice to those who suffer injustice, and sufficient to the needy. May we live in peace and harmony.

'Our Father, our Mother, who art in heaven, hallowed be thy name. Thy kingdom come. Thy will be done on earth as it is in heaven. Give us this day our daily bread, and forgive us our trespasses as we forgive those who trespass against us. And lead us not into temptation, but deliver us from evil. Amen.'

Mrs Cameron spent much of her day watching the street from her window. Her daughter visited her seldom, her sons never. Too busy with their families and their businesses. She didn't mind; she kept herself busy.

Eileen brought her a small dog. Mrs Cameron frowned.

'What's this then? Will it make a mess?'

'Her name is Minnie and she needs a home.'

Minnie sat on her haunches, gazed up at Mrs Cameron, and smiled. Their friendship was cemented with a bone.

Eileen remembered her black cat, Jules, who had always slept on her bed. Gregory had suggested putting a white ribbon around its neck and taking it with her when she entered. 'One more cat will go unnoticed.'

Clare brought her a photo of Jules curled up on her bed one visiting day. Every three months, four times a year, her family was allowed to visit her. She looked forward eagerly to seeing them, yet missed them so much when they had gone that she wished she hadn't seen them. There was much to tell and little to say. She felt closer to them than ever, but couldn't share the community's daily concerns with them. Neither could she feel as deep an anxiety over the resurfacing of the patio as did her father.

She entertained them in the parlour, sitting upright in her chair in emulation of the saintly Thérèse. She couldn't share the afternoon tea, as it was forbidden to eat or drink in front of outsiders. She explained that now the community was her spiritual family and that she had to submit to the discipline of convent life. 'A bit like being purged in a furnace.'

Her father spluttered into his tea. 'Need to turn the heaters up a bit if that's what you're intending. God, how do the old girls cope with the draughts?'

Her mother frowned at his blasphemy and asked her if she was always warm enough. 'You are happy, darling, aren't you? You wouldn't let pride stop you coming home if that's what you really wanted?' Her mother's grey eyes rounded with the effort of inquiring without seeming to intrude.

She didn't really care if she was a bit hot or cold. She missed playing tennis and swimming and sitting curled up in the big armchair at home reading a book. She missed going for walks on a summer evening or wandering through the bush on a blustery autumn day. She cried a little when her parents left and hoped that Mother Eleanor didn't notice her reddened eyes.

For Sister Celine she had a special love. Some Saturdays she would walk around the garden helping her choose the flowers for the statue of Our Lady. Celine told her about growing up in the country, the eldest of nine children. 'Those brothers of mine, they were always up to mischief. They tried my poor mother's patience, I can tell you. We worked hard in those days, and we were poor but we didn't think about it much. Everyone we knew worked hard.'

She would stand, secateurs in hand, gazing at the rose bush but seeing . . . what?

Eileen waited.

'Thanks be to God my two brothers came back from the war. Lots didn't, you know. Their guardian angels must have been very busy.'

Poverty she didn't mind much, chastity didn't trouble her unduly, although she had to admit to a certain curiosity about sex, but obedience — that was the difficult one.

Eileen is a sturdy, independent-minded young lady who should succeed in any chosen career.

That was before she entered. Suddenly she was lacking in

humility, lacking in docility, and not lacking in obstinacy.

Mother Eleanor was patient. 'If there was a person who never told a lie, never stole, never sinned against holy purity, and always obeyed the rules of the church, would you say that person was perfect?'

Eileen supposed you'd have to say he or she was very close to perfection.

'No, child. No! That person may not love God. Remember St Paul's epistle. To do all that without charity and love of God is empty. Learn to really love God and all else will follow. That is your path to happiness, and, God willing, to holiness. We'll get some surprises at the Last Judgment. Not everyone who cries 'Lord, Lord' will be there in the front row. You mark my words', she would add in the same voice she used when predicting victory for her favourite football team.

Eileen believed in hell, but she wasn't sure if there was anybody in it. Except Hitler.

One day she told Mother Eleanor that she always had a sense of God being with her, like a good friend. Mother Eleanor said that it was good to be in a state of grace and mindful always of God's presence. On the other hand, there was no virtue in inventing a God who was an extension of one's own personality, chatting to it, and then imagining you had spent the day in prayerful awareness. In spite of this admonition, Eileen did chat to Jesus. She told him about her feelings, her fears, and her sorrow at her lapses from holy rule. She told him about her homesickness and how she found the habit restricting and uncomfortable. Not that I am complaining, she would add hastily. She felt especially close to God when she was gardening. 'God must love us to give us such beautiful flowers', was all Sister Celine said when she told her.

Clare came to see her the day after she received the letter. Alan had gone to America for postgraduate study and had fallen in love with the daughter of his professor. They had been married almost immediately, and he was sure that Clare would understand and wish them well.

She didn't.

Eileen tried to soothe her as she sobbed in loud, painful gulps. She hugged her tightly until the spasms subsided, and she prayed for the right words to say.

'Mum will be glad, anyway', Clare finally said. 'Perhaps I should be a nun too. That would make her ecstatic.'

Her mother worried about the strained, withdrawn Clare, who

no longer sang around the house. She finished her degree with creditable results, did her Diploma of Education, and went teaching at the school where she and Eileen had been pupils. Predictability incarnate. She was toying with the idea of becoming a lay missionary when she met Ted at a meeting of the Young Catholic Workers.

Clare and Ted adopted the practice of saying the rosary when they were on a date together, hoping it would keep them pure. Mostly it did. Their honeymoon was somewhat of an ordeal. Clare giggled at the sight of Ted's green, striped pyjamas, and played with the hairs on his chest. Ted, who had felt moved by the intimacy and romance of the moment, was offended. They drank champagne in bed, cuddled a little, and went to sleep. Next morning they were the last in to breakfast, greeted by the indulgent smiles of all who noticed them. They, too, were smiling and ate little. Ted wanted to continue the practice of reciting the rosary just before going to bed, this time as a family prayer. Clare found it made her feel a bit inhibited later, as if a not quite approving God was watching them. She imagined she'd enjoy sex more when they returned to their flat near the university.

'If you conceive, we'll manage. You don't really need to work now you are married. I'm here to provide for the family.'

Clare forlornly examined her temperature graph. 'We could at least try. I'm very regular.'

'It's really a moral issue', said Ted. 'We should only use the rhythm method if the seriousness of the situation warrants it. I'm not sure that the church would consider your teaching career a serious matter. Besides, I don't want to go to bed with a thermometer.'

Clare muttered something which sounded suspiciously like 'Who cares about the church?' and wished momentarily that she had never married. She wished she was home with her parents. She even envied Eileen, who had no impediment to her studies. Ted tickled her toes and gave her his cute, little-boy smile, which his mother claimed to find irresistible. 'I'm so proud to have you as my wife.'

They didn't discuss the matter any more that night. Discussion did, however, play an important part in their lives. Both belonged to the Newman groups set up by the university chaplain, and Clare sat proudly one year while Ted delivered a paper on the True Nature of the Student Apostolate at a national seminar. Published later in a book of conference papers, it was promptly forgotten by all but Ted.

When three years went by without a sign of pregnancy Clare's mother suggested a novena to St Gerard Majellan. This was followed by prayers to the Infant Jesus of Prague, St Anne, and finally St Joseph of Cupertino. In the end it was a minor adjustment to Ted's reproductive apparatus which wrought the miracle. Almost five years to the day when they were married, their first son was born.

Clare wanted to call him Ambrose, as she admired the ancient bishop, but Ted's family insisted that all the first sons for generations back had been called Edward. Edward Ambrose sounded a bit pretentious for a tiny baby, as did Edward Francis, Edward Augustine, or even Edward Thomas. Did they have to call him Edward? He was christened Edward John. A year later Luke Ambrose was born, and fifteen months after that Elizabeth Ann.

Humanae Vitae, once a non-issue, raged about the kitchen. Most of Clare's friends were following their consciences and saving their marriages. After her fourth pregnancy ended in a miscarriage, Clare told Eileen that she thought the church was wrong about contraception. Eileen felt sad for her, and understood. It wasn't always easy to stick to your principles.

'What's so noble about getting pregnant all the time? I've got to the stage where I don't want Ted near me. What sort of a marriage is that? The church is sure to change its tune in time. They did finally admit that the earth moves around the sun. A bold step forward that was. You'll see, in a few years they'll be peddling the pill at the back of the church, next to the rosary beads and holy pictures. It's not all it's cracked up to be, you know', said Clare vehemently.

'What isn't?'

'It. Sexual intercourse. At least not for women. I think men seem to get a bit more out of it.'

Eileen loved community life, but she wondered what it would be like to have a husband. Someone who looked after you and protected you. As her father did her mother. Or like Ted and Clare.

'Ted's all right', Clare would say, 'but never marry an only son. They're spoilt from the cradle.'

'I don't intend to marry one — not this week anyway', she replied. Eileen thought back to that conversation later, when Clare told her that she and Ted had finally separated.

Jesus was an only son, she remembered, and she was the bride of Christ. Mother Eleanor told her and Anne not to get too fanciful about it. Sister Celine's favourite story was about the time she and

Sister Thecla had been travelling on a train one evening. There were two drunk men in the carriage. One had looked at the nuns in their black and white habits and demanded of the other: 'Who are they then?'

They're God's girls', the other had replied.

The first man looked at them even more closely and then announced: 'God can have them'.

Sister Celine laughed heartily every time she told the story.

Clare and Eileen's mother hadn't known anything about sex when she married. On her wedding night she had climbed into bed, given a happy yawn, said goodnight, and gone to sleep.

'What happened then?' Clare once asked her. Their mother simply smiled and said something about their father being a good man and a true gentleman. Something must have happened eventually.

Eileen had never been in love. Not really. She had been crazy about Gerard Armstrong, who was eighteen and had a girlfriend, from the time she was fourteen. The day he left for national service was a black day for her. Then there was Bernie, sports captain at the Christian Brothers College. He was fun, even when he showed off. They had danced together so much at a school social that Brother Brendan had arranged three progressive barn dances in a row.

Chapter Five

Pauline never entered a room, she arrived. A basket of books flung to the floor, she slumped into a chair and ran her hand through her hair. End of school year. Release of tension.

'Eileen, listen to this! The end-of-year mass. What a shemozzle! Georgina and her little group wanted plainsong. Plainsong! Her father is an academic. Tracey's guitar group had been practising all their rousing togetherness numbers for ages and weren't prepared to step down. Then, of course, there was my flute solo going begging. The Society for the Restoration of Decent Music in the Liturgy sat itself in the porch of the chapel and refused to go in. You can imagine Rosea wasn't too excited with parents stepping over them and Georgina rushing around handing out literature which she had run off — on our photocopier, I might add. Glorious compromise came to the rescue, with guitars at the beginning and end of mass, plainsong in the middle, and my flute after communion. I must admit the plainsong was rather soothing, especially after the folk hymns. Thank heavens Georgina won't be back next year. Rose was furious about the whole thing, until some parents congratulated her on the excellent catholic choice of music.'

Dusk. The street settled. Anne arrived, white and tired. Her turn to cook. She moved about the kitchen looking distant and uninvolved. The *Poulet au Verjus* she produced was superb, although she ate practically none.

Pauline was going to an end-of-year staff party, undecided as to whether she should wear lipstick — not necessary, but it brightened her up a bit, although not many women under forty wore make-up nowadays, unless they wore a lot. In the end she decided she'd feel a bit self-conscious and didn't. She still remembered the furore when a nun, the principal of the local parish primary school, had dyed her hair. Revving the car more than necessary, she backed down the driveway. Eileen wished that she wasn't going out, leaving her alone with Anne, then felt guilty.

She and Anne went back a long time together. As newly professed nuns they had been expected to do the convent washing before they left for university. This was designed to keep them humble, but only succeeded in making them sleepy during afternoon lectures. The order wasn't used to the idea of their members pursuing tertiary studies, and if the bishop hadn't insisted that they become qualified teachers they would not have been at the university. Bishop or no bishop, if they hadn't won scholarships they wouldn't have been there at all.

Anne soon left teaching. She escaped into researching the history of the first hundred years of the order in Australia. Entitled *A Time to Sow,* it was historically accurate but somewhat dull. Yet the life of those pioneer nuns was far from mundane. They worked under very difficult conditions, sweltering in their unsuitable attire, teaching large classes, living in inadequate accommodation, and given scant recognition for their efforts by the clergy, many of whom took male superiority as fundamental dogma. No wonder some of those women had become soured and bitter. The miracle was they didn't all end up that way.

'It makes you angry', Eileen suddenly said to Anne.

'Yes?'

'Those really early churchwomen: Hildegard, Brigid, and some of those wise, strong abbesses. How can we have allowed ourselves to become so subjugated?'

'Do you want a sociology lecture or agreement?' She picked up her book from the arm of the chair. 'I'll tell you what makes me angry.'

'What?'

'Your parishioners leaving notes in the Advent wreath. It's meant to be a symbol, not a repository for messages.'

Eileen went to her room and prepared her report on the catechetical program for that year.

Motherhood did not suit Karen. She kept the weight she put on during pregnancy and her skin and hair looked oily. Aaron grew into a blotchy, fretful baby. Amber-Mae's elf-like beauty came as a fresh surprise each time Eileen saw her. Had she had a daughter she would have liked her to look like that.

Aaron cried while Amber-Mae pushed and rocked his pram. He hiccupped, snorted, and snuffled, and finally went to sleep. Karen sat at the kitchen table, cigarette in hand, gazing at the latest electricity account with the same surprised despair with which she perused any bill. The whole life-experience was beyond her. She floundered like a beached whale, defying her would-be rescuers to achieve the impossible. Eileen felt inadequate. She listened to an involved story about neighbours whom Karen was going 'to get back at sometime'. Then Eileen gave details of a child-care centre established for unemployed single mothers who wanted to learn typing.

'Gawd', with a long sigh and exhalation of smoke, 'I should do something like that. I'd like a part-time job.'

A rearrangement of bulk on the kitchen chair and re-examination of the electricity bill. Eileen wanted to tell her to brush her hair.

Amber-Mae walked with her to the gate. 'My friend has a black, fluffy cat called Lucia and she has kittens. I'm not allowed to have one. Mummy says they make a mess.'

In which case the kitten would feel very much at home, Eileen thought, looking around. She bent down and gave the little girl a hug. As she walked to the car there were tears in her eyes.

Christmas. The church glowed with candle light and the promise of Christ come into the world. Even sinners rejoiced at Christmas. Eileen had always loved midnight mass. Now she sat with Pauline and Anne, singing 'The First Nowell' as they waited for the mass to begin. Behind the altar was a large poster, HAPPY BIRTHDAY, JESUS, written in letters formed from pieces of Christmas card. It had taken them four sessions at the Sunday school, much glue, and extraordinary patience to have it ready in time. Sister Josephine would have judged it untidy, possibly irreverent. She always organised the Corpus Christi procession, and pity help any girl who failed to turn up dressed exactly as directed in a white dress, long white socks, white shoes, and a white veil fashioned with white satin at the top. They had carried baskets filled with rose petals, which they kissed and threw on the ground, forming a carpet for the priest, who followed bearing the blessed sacrament in the gold monstrance. The church in the grey dawn light was full of incense. Pure soprano voices sang *Pangae Lingua*. The church knew how to put on a good show in those days.

The children had met during the morning to help her build the crib. One of the fathers had donated a bale of straw. The children placed their toy animals around the crib. The Bible didn't specifically mention a giraffe, Snoopy, three koalas, or a dog with a tartan nose being present at Bethlehem, but then it doesn't say they weren't. The crib figures, large plaster statues, had been part of the parish Christmas for as long as Eileen could remember. Five children adorned with tea towels, representing shepherds, wriggled and distracted. The three wise kings were held in check by the responsibility of holding their presents intact.

Music was provided by the liturgy group, which had assembled an extraordinary assortment of instruments too loudly amplified.

'Silent Night' was never meant to sound quite like that. The priest, facing his errant flock on what was for many their annual visit to mass, gave them a year's worth of sermon.

'Go in peace. The mass is ended, and a happy and holy Christmas.'

They emerged into the warm night. Goodwill and cheer prevailed. That was their community celebration. Each went her way for Christmas Day.

They exchanged presents before they went to bed.

'We're as bad as the children', Eileen said.

'I used to love Christmas when I was a kid.'

'So did I', said Pauline. 'All the bustle and cooking smells. The Christmas tree with lights! And feeling absolutely disgustingly full after dinner.'

Anne said nothing.

The next morning was something of a rush with all going separate ways. Eileen was to call on Mrs Cameron and Karen before going to Clare's for a family Christmas dinner. Ted wouldn't be there, of course. He and Clare had split up, and Ted now lived with a young woman called Kimberley. They'd even managed to produce a baby.

Anne always went back to the old convent on Christmas Day, although this time she was not staying for dinner. She had been invited by her professor and his wife to join them in their festivities. Pauline always spent her Christmas Day with her mother, who was now in an old people's home. She entertained them later with hilarious stories of the old dears and their antics, although not all the stories were funny.

Mrs Cameron was dressed and ready to go to her daughter's house. She peered anxiously through the window when she heard the car, and even had the ingratitude to look a little disappointed when she saw it was Eileen. Minnie was ready to go as well, with a tartan bow around her neck, a decoration she far from appreciated.

'Happy Christmas.'

Exchange of kisses and exchange of presents. Eileen had made Mrs Cameron a kneeling pad to ease her time in the garden. She had made herself one as well to ease the time she helped her. She opened the gaily wrapped parcel Mrs Cameron gave her while Mrs Cameron looked at her anxiously. She smiled when Eileen thanked her warmly. A box of handkerchiefs, a present from her grandchildren several years ago. Had she had a perpetual cold she could not have used up all the handkerchiefs her family had given her.

Karen's house had a look more of weariness than neglect. Karen's strident voice could be heard even as Eileen walked up the pathway. 'For Gawd's sake, Amber-Mae, let me get some sleep. Piss off.'

Amber-Mae came out through the front door, crying. She cheered up immediately when she saw Eileen. They sat down together on the top step.

'Do you know whose birthday it is today?' Eileen asked the little girl.

'Jesus', she answered proudly. 'Did you bring me a present?'

'Why should I do that? It isn't your birthday.'

Amber-Mae giggled in happy confidence that at least one of the parcels that Eileen carried was for her. She was right. Eileen had overcome her feminist ideals and brought her a small doll dressed in a layette knitted by Eileen's mother, who took a keen interest in stories of Amber-Mae. 'Poor little thing', she sighed. 'It's not much of a life for her. How is she going to turn out?'

'Like her mother, I suppose.'

Amber-Mae ran inside, holding her doll triumphantly. She, too, had a baby.

Aaron showed no respect for Karen's hangover and wailed incessantly. He was very wet. Karen resignedly walked out of the bedroom, shutting the door behind her, but not quickly enough to prevent Eileen seeing that she had not been alone. Thank goodness Aaron was still being breastfed. There were some Christmas presents Karen could do without.

'Happy Christmas, Karen.'

She did not kiss her. Eileen had to admit that she found Karen's fat bulk physically repulsive. She found her lethargy and indolence irritating and her treatment of her children distressing. She could think of several reasons why she should not feel so negatively towards a woman whom Jesus undoubtedly loved and for whom he had died, but reason had little effect on her emotions.

Karen held her hand to her head and muttered: 'Gawd I feel awful. Sorry, Sister. Happy Christmas to you. Would you like a drink or something?' She gestured ineffectually towards the refrigerator.

'No thanks, Karen. I am just on my way to my sister's place.'

A sudden thought. 'Amber-Mae would be very welcome. Would you allow me to take her with me?'

Amber-Mae knew she was under discussion but wasn't quite sure what it was all about. She sidled up to Eileen and took her hand.

The gesture nearly deprived her of her Christmas visit, but Karen eventually sighed and said: 'Okay by me. You can have Aaron too if you like.' An offer which Eileen declined.

'Who's your little friend?' Clare, wearing an apron, her face moist with sweat, stood on the front path. She was carrying a bunch of freshly cut roses.

'Amber-Mae. This is my sister Clare. You can call her Aunty Clare.'

'Just Clare will do. Come in, both of you.'

Amber-Mae, wide-eyed, held Eileen's hand.

Clare looked at her a little more closely. 'How would you like a bath? I can make you some beaut bubbles.'

The little girl, her shampooed hair peaked into a cocky's crest, laughed at herself in the mirror. Rainbows bibbled around the rim of the bath.

Clare found her fresh clothes donated for the women's refuge, and Eileen rinsed out Amber-Mae's offending underwear and dress, hanging them out to dry.

Edward, Luke, and Elizabeth sat on the lounge floor surrounded by wrapping paper and lollies. It was a hot day. They watched with great interest as Clare, with a few deft movements, created order where chaos had reigned. Eileen offered to help peel vegetables and set the table. Cheerful chirping sounds from the front verandah. Their parents had arrived. Eileen's mother kissed both her daughters and nodded brightly at her grandchildren. Presents were exchanged, shrill exclamations mingled with mumbled thanks. Adolescence resumed normal apathy. Amber-Mae blossomed to the verge of showing off, and had to be calmed with a story read by Eileen's mother. A festooned Christmas tree stood in one corner and a small plastic crib had pride of place on the mantelpiece. 'Mum likes it', Clare explained to Eileen, who needed no explanation. 'She won't be with us forever, and I can't see it does any harm.'

Eileen wondered if the crib were solely for their parents' benefit. Had Clare really discarded her faith? Clare, who had organised discussion groups and liturgy meetings in those first heady days of Vatican II. Clare had outshone most of the nuns in her enthusiasm then. Now she was the consummate atheist. No lukewarm agnosticism for our Clare.

An acceptable meal. Amber-Mae ate little because she was shy and unused to food other than hamburgers, fish fingers, and chips.

Eileen's mother had supplied the Christmas pudding and her dad had concocted the brandy sauce. Would it be Christmas without that ritual? As her parents did the dishes Eileen looked at them fondly.

Adolescence had retired to another room to watch television. Lazy lumps! Both Ted and Clare had had very definite ideas about bringing up children, but unfortunately their ideas did not coincide. In the resulting confusion three selfish, self-centred young people emerged. Or perhaps they were just normal young people. Who can remember what she was like at that age?

Christmas dinner produces a wonderful feeling of wellbeing and drowsiness, even in those who have eaten little. Amber-Mae curled up on the old couch on the verandah and went fast asleep, holding her doll in her arms.

'She must be tired', said Clare. 'They rarely put themselves to bed. You see them at the refuge, fighting sleep until the bitter end. I think they are frightened that something terrible will happen once they stop watching.'

The sisters sat on the shady verandah. The front lawn looked dry and neglected, although not totally unkempt. Sister Celine's fingers would have itched to weed the rose garden, Eileen thought. Clare dozed.

The sun blazed, tempered by a cool breeze. The whole street echoed the hush which had descended on the house. Only faint sounds of quarreling came from the family room. The boys could never reconcile themselves to the fact that Elizabeth usually beat them at eight ball.

Ted was spending the day with 'that woman', as Clare called her, and their new baby. She felt no jealousy, only sympathy.

'Those meek and mild wifey types are the sort who end up in the women's refuge.'

'I can't see Ted hitting a woman.'

'He hit me once.'

'What did you do?'

'Hit him back.'

'No, before he hit you.'

'Doesn't matter what I did. He had no right to hit me.'

Eileen offered to make a cup of tea.

Amber-Mae woke up and devoured a glass of milk and a turkey sandwich. Flushed from sleep, her hair shiny, she looked like an old-fashioned fairy, apart from a slight nervous twitch, which Karen tried to cure her of by slapping her, a remedy which had no effect.

Eileen's mother asked her to stroll around the garden, as she knew she would. She asked her if Clare had gone to midnight mass with her, as she knew she would. The answer produced a sigh.

'What is wrong with that girl? She used to be so devout. I don't know what Sister Leo would say if she knew Clare didn't go to mass any more.'

'Probably pray for her.'

'Maybe I should tell her, then. Clare is certainly at the top of my list.'

Eileen's mother, erect, precise in her movements, had a kindly face. At this moment she looked distressed.

'Do you know what I think it is?' she continued immediately. 'I think it was all those home masses. You lose respect when you are all sitting around making up things as you go along. It wasn't special any more.'

'Clare thought they were special. Both she and Ted. They put a lot of work into their liturgy group. I could do with a few like that in our parish.'

'Well, pray for her, dear. I know she isn't happy. Not really. She couldn't be.'

'Who couldn't be happy?' Clare had just joined them.

'You, dear.'

'Nonsense. I'm perfectly happy, except for a few lacks, which any rich man could supply.'

'I thought you were off men', said Clare's mother.

'One has to make sacrifices.'

Why does she always hide behind flippancy? Eileen thought. We are her family. Can't she talk honestly to us at least?

Her mother sighed and said it was time to go home, woke her husband, and walked down the path looking slightly defeated. Clare felt guilty and relieved at the same time.

Eileen thought of Anne enjoying her dinner with the professor and his wife. It would have been the first time since she entered that she had not spent Christmas Day with the community. Had she come to feel that the academic world was her community?

Every Christmas the professor invited one waif or stray, usually a visiting student or junior lecturer, to Christmas dinner as a witness to the world that he understood the Christmas message. The recipients of the professor's Christian charity fell either into the Song of Songs category or that of an earnest seeker of the truth. After an appraising glance the professor's wife greeted Anne warmly.

Anne stopped feeling guilty about not spending the day with the old nuns when she entered the professor's house. It was a house in harmony; worldliness and spirituality were reconciled. St Francis, where are you now? she thought.

Was it at that moment that she decided to leave the order? Marriages don't break up in a day. Her vocation was not 'lost'. It had become irrelevant.

That evening, with uncharacteristic animation, she told Eileen and Pauline about her day. 'The house was full of treasures. They collect things', she explained, not realising that she was being added to the collection. 'Not ostentatious showy stuff, but all the things Adrian and Christine have brought back from their travels. They lived in the Holy Lands for three years while he was working on his thesis. How I envy them! What really impressed me was a huge brass plate inscribed with passages from the Koran. You would have appreciated that, Eileen, seeing you do yoga.'

Eileen acknowledged both the irrelevancy and pertinence of that comment.

'And the meal!' Anne continued. 'I am not, as you know, a greedy woman, but that meal was exquisite. Not traditional English Christmas fare. Or not our sisters' version of it. How often have you had marinated calamari on Christmas Day? That was the entree. The main course was what Christine described as an adaptation of a Lebanese recipe she had learnt while they lived in Beirut. That was before all the trouble really flared up. It was all so civilised. These people have given their lives to God without having to flagellate themselves daily.'

Neither Pauline nor Eileen quite saw the connection between international cuisine and eulogising of the professor's personal philosophy, but then they hadn't tasted the dessert.

Pauline's had been a mundane Christmas dinner. Not a truffle in sight, she complained. The only excitement was when the Christmas tree started to smoulder because one of the lights overheated, and she had quenched the flames while her mother looked on, smiling vaguely, and saying 'That's nice, dear' when it was all over.

'I love my mother', Pauline said, 'but it is good to be home'.

Eileen didn't mention Amber-Mae. She tried not to talk about her revolting niece and nephews, but exasperation overcame charity. Then she told them about Clare's work at the women's shelter. Even on Christmas Day there had been an emergency, and Clare had had to go down and sort it out. Someone had forgotten about peace and goodwill and was hurling stones and abuse at the house while his wife and children cowered inside.

They prayed together, each with her thoughts, then retired to bed.

Eileen couldn't sleep. Too much food perhaps. Amber-Mae had drawn back and grabbed at her hand as they had walked up the front steps. Karen had greeted them warmly enough. Aaron, for once, seemed dry and fed and was asleep. Eileen kept thinking of the way Clare had looked at Amber-Mae and said: 'I've seen that one before. They don't have much chance, do they?'

How would Sister Josephine have reacted? She could only relate to deserving poor, preferably Irish and Catholic. She would have had little sympathy for Karen, and her only solution for Amber-Mae would have been a Catholic orphanage with the good nuns. Like herself? Sister Celine would have swept Amber-Mae into her arms and called her a poor little thing. Then there would have been a trip to the pantry and Amber-Mae would have emerged clutching a biscuit with one hand and Sister Celine with the other. But she would have been powerless to offer more. Today's nuns were more practical. She had taken the little girl away for the day. And brought her back.

I do find your world difficult, Jesus, although it is much as you left it. Why did you allow poverty, hunger, sickness, and prejudice to continue? You could see all the pain. She acknowledged this as simplistic nonsense. Jesus, the grand vizier, waves his magic wand and cures all ills.

But why Amber-Mae? Why should such a loving, trusting little girl have so little chance? Had Karen been a loving, trusting little girl once?

God, she prayed, can't something be done about Amber-Mae? She talked to Jesus, but prayed about serious things to God. Her theology was sound. She knew that God the Son, Jesus Christ, was equal to God the Father, but in her human understanding of this great mystery it seemed as though God was the big boss and Jesus was the one who understood. How could she talk to a being who was omnipotent, omniscient, and omnipresent? Awe-inspiring, but a bit remote. Jesus, who had experienced hunger, sore feet and backaches, understood. He had wept.

What if Jesus had been born a woman? That thought raised endless possibilities as she drifted off to sleep at last.

Chapter Six

Anne's thoughts were troubled. Seduction by the suburbs? Civilised society? In her academic world Anne had no doubts that society was civilised. Would God love her less if she lived in a small unit near the university and became a senior lecturer in the theology department? She could even do some good.

'You Roman Catholics still regard High Church Anglicans as poor relations', Adrian had chided her. 'I like to think history is on their side. They do have apostolic succession.'

Anne's special area was medieval mysticism. She didn't buy into the professor's argument. She must be the only totally sexless woman I have met, thought the professor as he poured Anne a glass of wine. Does she loosen up with alcohol?

Not much.

'Let's forget the Inquisition', Christine said, frowning. She wondered if Anne would look better in an old-fashioned habit. The sort of half-this-and-half-that nuns now wore didn't do a thing for any of them.

Anne had admired the family photo album, offered to wash up (an offer definitively refused), and listened with appreciation to Bach's Christmas Oratorio. Neither Adrian nor Christine suspected her turmoil.

Pauline and Eileen did when she talked about leaving them.

'Ask for a year off', Pauline advised. 'That way you can come back without a lot of hoo-ha.'

Anne promised to think about it and make a decision by Easter. An appropriate time for a new beginning, in whatever direction.

When alone, Pauline and Eileen discussed it.

'How will she live?'

'On her salary, very nicely thank you.' Pauline sounded waspish.

'How will we manage on your salary and my parish contribution? Do you think we should ask Anne for maintenance?'

Pauline wondered if the parish could increase Eileen's allowance, but Eileen felt that the weekly envelopes had gone as far as they were going.

'Could we get in another sister?' Pauline asked.

'Who? There were twenty of us in the two years of our novitiate, and now there are three. Two, if Anne goes. So much for invigoration and renewal. Vatican II has a lot to answer for. We'll manage. I did not become a nun to spend sleepless nights over money.'

Pauline suddenly laughed. 'Sister Josephine would advise us to pray, and while we were finishing the rosary there would be a knock at the door: a wealthy businessman with a large donation to help our work. Didn't you love her stories?'

Eileen had loved her stories and believed each one implicitly. This was because Sister Josephine believed them. And who is to say they were not true? Her favourite was the orphanage story, where the nuns and orphans prayed because they were starving and had no money for food. As they prayed, a knock came at the door. A man asked if they could use some milk from his herd of cows, which he was taking along the road to his new farm. Warm, fresh milk was better than nothing to a starving orphan. Nowadays it would be a pizza delivery van, which broke down in front of the building.

'God is not mocked', she said to Pauline. 'We'll manage.'

Clare had money problems at the women's refuge. Hurting women and children weren't voting strength, a fact which was reflected in the government grants. Maybe they should export them. Clare wrote submissions, sought sponsors, and occasionally begged. She didn't think of praying.

Anne concentrated on her thesis and lectures and said no more about leaving. Eileen worried that Anne's obsession with mysticism was unhealthy. Anne hardly ate, becoming gaunter by the day.

'Why don't you exercise?' she said. 'It's healthier than starving to death and just as good for the soul.'

Even so, she couldn't see Anne with her pin-legs and severe expression jogging around the local park.

Sometimes they talked. Anne's passion was for Catherine of Siena, a saint for whom Eileen felt little. 'She developed a cult of nothingness. Just sat in her attic weeping for her non-existent sins and writing interfering letters. On top of that she left her mother to do all the housework.'

Anne laughed. 'Don't talk about things you know little about. Catherine was a great saint and a doctor of the church. If you want to trivialise, you could say that your famous Teresa of Avila did nothing but roam around the countryside being rude to God and interfering.'

'At least we agree they were interferers. So was Hildegard. That's why we aren't great saints — we mind our own business', said Eileen.

Even Anne had to admit that Margery Kempe of Lynn was a little extreme. She was at her happiest when she was most sad.

'You have to see it all in context, though', Anne said. As Anne drew in a long breath, Eileen said she had to go. She was vitally interested in Anne's peace of mind, but not in hearing one of her lectures.

Mrs Cameron had caught a bad cold, which refused to go away. She looked old and frail. Minnie slept at her feet a lot while Mrs Cameron dozed in her comfortable cane chair, a shawl around her shoulders. There wasn't a great deal of gardening done, although she fretted at the sight of the weeds and overgrown bushes. Eileen spent one morning there doing what she could while Mrs Cameron sat on the front verandah feebly protesting and coughing.

It was Pauline who made the suggestion and Sister Monica from the local primary school who agreed. For a month four grade six boys arrived each Thursday afternoon and weeded, planted, tidied up, and played with Minnie. Mrs Cameron supplied the cordial, biscuits, and delighted smile. Her own children were relieved when they heard of this arrangement. Even when her cough was better the boys still came, because they had grown fond of the old lady. And it was better than lessons. Minor crisis when one of the parents protested that his boy would be better doing extra arithmetic than pulling up weeds. He sent his boy to a Catholic school to get a good education. Christian charity he could learn at home.

Sister Monica bowed to parental pressure and stopped the weekly working-bees.

'Give us this day our daily bread, and forgive us our trespasses as we forgive those who trespass against us . . . When is Anne going to tell us what she is thinking? . . . Amen.'

Their evening devotions finished. Eileen found her praying more and more distracted lately. It didn't come from the heart. Or it did, but it didn't feel right. She wasn't sure what she should feel. Prayer is an act of will, a communication with God, not a warm, fuzzy feeling. She liked to think that God understood, but maybe he was disappointed in her and was marking down subtotals on her heavenly balance sheet. Often now she found herself returning to her childish way of thinking about God and religion. Even while she laughed at herself she wondered. As a small child she used to picture her soul as a white cotton reel which became smudged every time she sinned. When it was covered in black marks she had no more grace. When her soul was full of grace it shone like the sun shining through the clouds. Then God was happy. Now she knew that God was perfect and so couldn't be unhappy, but she didn't believe it. Her inner heart told her that he was saddened by the evil that people did, the suffering in the world caused by mismanagement of the world's resources.

All this because Anne couldn't make up her mind, or couldn't feel trusting enough in their sensitivity to confide in them. Pauline and Eileen tried not to discuss it — or not often. Pauline said that Anne was making sure they did penance for Lent, but she would have been quite happy to give up smoking, as usual. Eileen found it hard to choose a suitable Lenten penance. Life was easier when the church obligated one to fasting and abstinence. Nowadays going without things was considered a bit unimaginative. Think positive, think of a meaningful penance. She could spend the whole forty days deciding something suitable.

Pauline found solace in her flute. Anne had once commented that she thought the tuba would have been more appropriate. Almost every night soft, gentle melodies, soothingly unobtrusive, could be heard from Pauline's room. It was the only time she stayed in the one place for more than two minutes. Eileen practised her yoga but found it hard to completely relax. She wished she could afford to go to classes and be guided by a guru. She suspected her asanas were all wrong and doing more harm than good.

Anne looked so thin they wondered if she was fasting for the whole of Lent.

It was Anne who suggested a retreat. A proper, old-fashioned retreat where they prayed and meditated in silence. None of this reaching out to each other, which she found distracting and distasteful.

Pauline, noted for her retreats, felt hurt. Eileen tactfully refrained from comment, although she had her opinion about the efficacy of modern retreats. She had seen too many students spend the afternoon session writing complimentary, supportive messages to each other and then continue their feuds in the evening with renewed vigour. Had that happened in early Christian communities, she wondered.

She nearly withdrew from the whole idea when they discovered the only priest available was Father Kendall. A retired Irish priest, without question pre-Vatican II, was not, on the surface, an ideal retreat master. Anne suggested they ask Adrian and Christine instead, Adrian to direct them and Christine to look after the cooking. While Eileen and Pauline felt they might accept a Protestant theologian, they drew the line at his wife making the sandwiches.

'Henry VIII has a lot to answer for', declared Eileen.
'Meaning?' asked Anne.
'Why break away? Sounds like nothing changed.'

Anne promised to leave her medieval mystics behind and read some more modern religious writing if Eileen promised to read some of the more prayerful ancients. Eileen had planned to reread the gospels. Was that prayerful and ancient enough? Pauline wanted to reread the Psalms. As they discussed and planned, the house began to feel warm and close again. Anne's face was animated as she hunted for a suitable book for Eileen, 'just in case'. One evening they spent choosing the readings for their retreat masses.

'Do you realise that we haven't been to mass together since Christmas except for two Sundays ago?' said Pauline.

Finding daily mass was sometimes a chore. Gone were the days when a convent full of nuns could command the presence each day of one of the parish priests to say mass for them. Gone were the days when they knelt down each morning to offer the sacrifice of Calvary anew and receive communion together. Now they found a mass where they could. Eileen usually during the day at the parish church, Pauline at school or the local cathedral, where she often saw Anne although they did not always kneel together.

The Sunday school would have to cope without Eileen for that weekend. She left notes and instructions, lots of textas and paper, a gramophone record of children's hymns, and an animated version of the day's gospel on video, fresh from America. She doubted that they would notice her absence.

Friday night they packed overnight bags, put on the telephone answering machine, and set off in the community car for the old convent. They stopped for tea at the Pizza Hut, feeling decadent and un-Lenten. The pizza gave them indigestion, which Eileen felt was a judgment.

The driveway to the old convent, now a seminar centre, hadn't changed much since her mother had driven her there on that first day. Green lawns were bordered by flower strips, and the trees were just beginning to get their autumn leaves. Eileen remembered the times she and Anne had had to sweep up the fallen leaves and take them in a wheelbarrow around to the compost heap. Sister Celine claimed that there was a lesson to be learnt from the fact that her compost produced beautifully scented roses which lasted long after others had faded. The Parable of the Roses according to Sister Celine. Eileen felt sure that its meaning had something to do with humility. In those days they were hot on humility and self-effacement. Quite out of touch with modern psychology. She wondered if the retreat to be run by dear old Father Kendall was going to be an absolute waste of time.

They were to be in the section where the two sisters, Rosaria and Immaculata, lived and worked as caretakers and sacristans for the centre. The two old nuns greeted them joyously.

'We know you have to keep silence for the retreat, but it doesn't really start until tomorrow, so we can have a good chat tonight', said Sister Rosaria as she helped them with their overnight bags and showed them where to park the car.

'We have prepared a little supper for you even though you said you would have tea before you came. You must be hungry after your journey', added Sister Immaculata.

All of ten kilometres, thought Eileen, who was still full of pizza.

A 'little supper' turned out to be a sumptuous spread. The two old nuns had had a wonderful afternoon baking. Eileen looked at the fairy cakes and apple turnovers and thought: Do I tell them I'm off cakes and sweets for Lent? She liked to think it was charity rather than greed which motivated her as she bit into a strawberry tart.

Pauline had no inhibitions and a healthy appetite.

Anne picked at one small cake, then slid it into the rubbish bin when nobody was looking.

'I know it is Lent, but I am sure God won't mind us celebrating your being here', said Sister Rosaria.

'Why do you all think of God as the ever-watchful policeman?' snapped Anne. And why do you talk about God all the time in such a limiting way? she thought to herself. At the university I mix with so many interesting people who discuss so many things. And go overseas. And go to the theatre and read all sorts of books and don't seem any the worse for any of it.

None of them answered her question. There was a short silence broken only by the sound of tea being poured into a cup. Pauline cut across the awkwardness with a bright 'This certainly is a lovely surprise. I haven't had such a lovely supper for a long time. You didn't indulge us like this when we were young nuns.'

They fell to talking about old times, the nuns who had left, and their doings. 'Jennifer is married now with a young family. Her husband is such a nice man. An ex-priest.' The last sentence spoken with a slight drop in tone. Sister Immaculata had not quite come to terms with ex-priests. Marian had become the matron of a large hospital, and several others were teaching around the state.

'There aren't many of us left, and no young ones to take our place', mourned Sister Rosaria. 'Do you think young people are more selfish nowadays?'

They washed up, and then all went to the chapel for night prayers. Eileen, Anne, and Pauline, in differing ways, felt moved to be back in the chapel with their community, saying night prayers and then going to bed in silence, a silence which they would not break for two days.

Eileen's bed was positioned so that she could see out of her window. Wonderfully peaceful, with no traffic noise, and at the far edge of the window she could just make out the edge of a mulberry tree. She didn't remember being able to see it years ago. This garden, the fruit of their labours, had flourished. Obviously symbolic, but of what she had not quite worked out when she fell asleep.

Next morning she awoke to pervading calm. Birds could be heard singing in the garden. No sound of cars or neighbours. It must be easy to be good and God-centred amid tranquillity. Why had they ever left this haven?

Why indeed? The short answer was Vatican II. The more complex one was years of upheaval and searching for a new way. A time of questioning, which for some became a time of doubting, then complete rejection. Vatican II had been a response to a great cry within the church for change. Eileen, secure in her convent, had been unaware of the stirrings. Those who now blamed Vatican II for all the laxity and waywardness they now perceived within the church probably hadn't known about it either. They had been secure with the Latin mass, daily rosary, and obedience to the magisterium of the church. For them the intoxication and excitement and searching represented anarchy, and in no way could the Holy Roman Catholic Apostolic Church live with anarchy. For them Vatican II represented betrayal.

Sister Celine had cried when told that Pius XII had died. 'Such a good man, a holy man, and a leader we could be proud of', she had said, tearing leaves off the roses in her distress.

They had prayed mightily for the repose of his soul at their morning masses and at a very grand affair at the cathedral, where all the clergy turned up in regalia. Eileen had felt that the nuns looked like little wrens next to the magnificence of the scarlet and violet of the higher clergy. No expense was spared for the costumes and props — but she had not thought like that in those days.

A caretaker pope. That was what they called John XXIII. A pious priest who would keep things ticking over for a few years. The cardinals who had voted for him had not known their man. In a short time he had turned their world a little topsy-turvy, opened the windows, as he put it, and let the Spirit flow through. The Spirit disturbed much more than a bit of dust in the corners. No-one was safe.

The old convent had really buzzed then. Who would have thought some of those old nuns had so much passion in them, especially when the length of their skirts was questioned? Thank God Sister Josephine had gone to her eternal rest. There would have been no rest for any of them had she been around at that time. To ask Sister Josephine to take her mission out into the world would have been unfair on both her and the world.

It was all very well the Second Vatican Council sending out from Rome instructions to religious orders all over the world to examine their way of living and change where necessary. Eileen had lived with some of the nuns for a number of years, but she found she didn't really know most of them. To change is painful. It involves acknowledging a lack of perfection, and perfection was what they were all striving for, their reason for choosing to be religious in the first place. It wasn't as simple as the younger nuns being for change and the older nuns against it. The convent split into two camps, with a number of factions within each camp. Christian charity was strained. Anne was against the changes to the liturgy, but they had no say in that. A new, stone altar was placed in front of the old decorated altar, which was right at the back of the church. Now it was 'theatre in the round'. The first time the priest said mass facing them Eileen felt intensely embarrassed, as though she was watching him perform some very private function. The priest looked selfconscious too, and had to keep referring to the book for the English words.

'Hundreds of years of tradition just thrown away', Anne mourned. 'And who wants to hear plainsong in English? It sounds so unpoetical.'

Plainsong became the least of their worries. New, folksy hymns, with trite sentiments, became the thing. Or, if you belonged to the new thinkers, they were songs of praise which expressed our feelings of loneliness, and our need for love, reassurance, and social justice. Thus they appealed to 'the people'. 'The people' had a lot to answer for, according to Anne.

'Who cares about relevancy?' she asked them at one soul-searching session. 'The church has been irrelevant for two thousand years. Why should it change now?' And before she could be denounced as a heretic, Reverend Mother added: 'Jesus was never concerned with relevancy. He brought a new law and a new freedom.'

'Exactly!' an advocate for great change cried in triumph. 'And all we are asking for is the freedom to live as Jesus wants. "I come so you can have life in abundance." That's what it is all about!'

Some nuns could not see how the length of their skirts or their veils were involved in all this discussion. 'Our veil', said one, 'is a symbol of our virginity'.

'Are you less a virgin if the veil is modified?' asked Eileen, but her frivolity was not appreciated.

'Think of the time it takes to launder the habits we wear', Sister Rosaria said. 'It's just not practical to keep them as they are. Why take a vow of poverty and then spend time and money on clothes which are so impractical?'

Who would have thought Sister Rosaria would come out with a statement like that? They were all silenced for a moment.

Eileen thought of all this as she went to the chapel for their first retreat mass next morning. Her feelings about peace and tranquillity became mixed as she met the others in the chapel for morning mass, carefully avoiding their eyes so that no personal communication could distract any of them. Would a good-morning smile really have shattered Anne's deep thoughts or distracted Pauline's impending meditation? She felt cranky and out of sorts, and missed her morning yoga. Later she might take a rug out under the trees, if there weren't people around. She didn't fancy a group of conferring teachers coming upon her standing on her head.

Father Kendall was even older than she remembered. He had an aura about him which she hoped was sanctity, not senility. He tottered about the altar but said the mass in a clear, steady voice.

Having given her support to Anne, who by now had completely forgotten that the idea for the retreat had come originally from her, she was very worried that it would be a fiasco. Pauline could cope, but the thought of Anne's accusing eyes and comments about how far behind she now was with her thesis because of losing a whole weekend bothered her. She's such an unhappy person, she thought, and yet she has so much to be thankful for. Dear Lord, help us to be grateful for the gifts you have given us.

Father Kendall was to give them a short talk after mass and leave them to their thoughts for the rest of the morning. They were spiritually mature enough to guide their reading and meditation effectively. Really they didn't need a priest at all, except for saying mass, and hearing their confessions if they so desired. Would women ever be given their rightful place in the order of things, Eileen wondered, and then dismissed the thought as distracting. She was here to examine her apostolate and to see how effectively she could bring God's word to his people.

'We took sweet counsel together and walked unto the house of God in company.' Father Kendall pronounced those words, and looked at them over his glasses. He took his glasses off, folded them, and held them in his hand with his Bible. Then he smiled at them. 'Sweet counsel it was to wish to devote a weekend solely to the Lord, and with each other.'

He spoke beautifully, yet none of them could later recall his words. What stayed with them was a consciousness of his goodness.

Anne stirred uneasily as she remembered her constant inner criticisms of almost everybody. Except Adrian and Christine, who shone like beacons in a crass, unthinking world. She had to be honest. She envied them, their way of life, and their being together.

Eileen felt guilty about so many things. Too often lately she had calculated the cost in time and energy before offering help.

Pauline was troubled. She was aware that she did not always live her vocation. It was so hard surrounded by secular colleagues.

Their breakfast was eaten in an uncomfortable silence. They were out of practice with that discipline. Pauline became terribly conscious of the sound of her munching, and swallowed a gulp of tea to soften the toast.

The morning was sunny and cool. They walked their separate ways in the garden, reading and thinking, as religious have done throughout the centuries. Eileen abandoned the idea of a yoga session. It didn't seem appropriate, and she was relaxed anyway. The rhythm of walking had accomplished that.

Pauline played her flute for a while, seated at the foot of the grotto. She might have been serenading Our Lady, or just enjoying the echo from the rocky walls. Either way it sounded serene and melodic. Eileen, hearing her, remembered how they used to put copies of their exam numbers under the rocks of the grotto at school. Sister Mary Magdalen assured them that without putting in the work, no amount of placing numbers in holy places would guarantee success in exams. Was it piety or superstition which had led them to these practices, she wondered, although she already knew the answer.

Anne settled in a large chair in the sun, opened a book, and, within minutes, was fast asleep. The sleep was exactly what she needed she decided when she awoke. Eileen noted that she ate a whole cake at afternoon tea. The pinched look about her eyes had eased. They had taken sweet counsel together. It was good that they were here. Had Anne reached a decision? Eileen half expected that she would tell them definitely after the retreat if she intended leaving the order.

Father Kendall's evening homily began with another quotation. 'Creation looks upon its creator like the beloved upon her lover.'

Eileen recognised the source as Hildegard of Bingen. What was Father Kendall doing reading Hildegard? She must ask him later what he thought about the ordination of women priests.

'All you that are righteous, shout for joy for what the Lord has done', Father Kendall continued, establishing his orthodoxy by quoting from the Psalms. He talked of people's responsibility to protect what God had given them, and he said 'man's responsibility' only once. They appreciated his efforts. The world was a terrible place, full of fear, famine, and violence. They were no strangers to human misery and loneliness. What were they doing, in God's name, about it?

The three nuns stared at Father Kendall, trying to see the relevance of his message in their everyday lives. Should they be more conscientious about recycling the garbage? Should they join more protest marches against nuclear arms?

He returned to the original theme, ' . . like the beloved upon her lover', and spoke so movingly about the love of God that Pauline was almost moved to tears. Eileen felt her awareness of God grow within her. She retired to her old cell aglow with a feeling akin to ecstasy. Before getting into bed she knelt and prayed.

By Sunday evening their sense of renewal, virtue, and good resolutions knew no limit. The final talk had concentrated on the gifts of the Holy Spirit, and they were reminded of John's words: 'God is Spirit, and they that worship him must worship him in spirit and in truth.'

Eileen preferred to think of God as a Spirit rather than a cosy uncle, which was where she felt some modern theologians were leading her. Before this retreat she had felt so sure that she knew her God. So sure that she really spoke to him or her in prayer. In spite of her liberated ideas she found it hard to think of God as 'she' and it seemed disrespectful to call God 'it'. Now she felt that she had not plumbed the depths of God's love for his people. She had not grasped the nature of God. Paradoxically she had not stilled her intermittent doubts. She knew that she could logically accept that there was no God. All belief was a gamble. Sometimes her doubts concerned the nature of God. What if it turned out that God was less than perfect? Was not all good, all powerful and all loving? Would that mean that her religious life was a sham? Maybe Mother Eleanor had been right when she said it was not good to think too much. 'The devil has a brilliant mind. He can twist and confuse your thoughts. It is better to have a simple faith and love God', she had once said. Eileen noted, in passing, that there was no move afoot to give the devil a feminine persona! She brought her thoughts back to the present, to Father's final comment.

'Remember that the greatest commandment of all is that you must love your God with all your heart and mind and soul. Seek the kingdom of God. Do not be afraid to suffer. The cross leads to the resurrection.'

He made it seem simple, what she had been striving for most of her life to achieve.

Eileen, Pauline, and Anne farewelled the two old nuns and drove back to their convent home. The car buzzed with goodwill.

Their euphoria didn't last long. On returning home they found that Anne had left the bathroom light on all weekend. At least Pauline said it was Anne, and Anne said she couldn't remember and it could have been any of them.

'Except', replied Pauline, 'you were the last one in the bathroom before we left'.

'It doesn't matter', soothed Eileen. 'One little globe doesn't burn that much electricity. It probably kept the burglars away.'

Anne was quite cheerful and outgoing for about three days then gradually slumped back into lethargy and depression. She may have been influenced by her study of medieval mysticism. In later years Anne told Eileen that she had believed that by living a life of extreme penance and fasting she would tread the path, if not to sanctity, at least to mystical experience. In her arrogance she hoped to wrest a vision or state of ecstasy from God. Nothing spectacular, no stigmata — but something. Eileen had replied that she thought the great saints were motivated by extreme love of God, not a desire for an experience, and that that may have had something to do with Anne's failure to achieve anything more noteworthy than fainting on the bus. Immediately she regretted her response. Barriers, always barriers. Learn to shut up occasionally, she told herself.

They had arrived home late in the afternoon. Within a short time the 'world' flooded back into their lives via the answering machine.

Adrian had the book Anne was looking for and would bring it to university on Monday.

The Sunday school teacher couldn't find the key to the cupboard with the hymnbooks and then rang later to say she hadn't realised that it wasn't locked, and everything had gone well.

One of Pauline's students couldn't understand her homework and went through several beeps on the machine enlarging on her stress and her inability to cope with life and question four of the topic.

Clare had a problem at the refuge which she thought Eileen might be able to help with and could she please ring back as soon as possible and where the hell was she and why was she never there when she was needed? Typical religious!

They were back on duty doing the Lord's work. All those years ago in Galilee had he thanked his Father that telephones and answering machines had not been invented?

Some of the peace of the retreat weekend remained with Eileen as she tidied her room and prepared for the coming week. She sat cross-legged on the floor, breathing in positive goodness and breathing out negativity. Slow, regular breathing. Into her mind came the words: 'Creation looks upon her creator like the beloved upon her lover'.

Years before, at the request of John XXIII, the community had questioned its role in the church. A request which led to the convening of Vatican II. This became the time of butcher's paper and lists written out in texta.

Their founder had been the only child, and therefore the heiress, in a rich family. She defied her father by refusing to marry her wealthy suitor. In the end, after a great deal of bullying on the father's side and prayers and patience on the daughter's, her father had come around and given her the money to buy an old house, which she turned into a school. Three friends joined her. They suffered privation, prejudice, and downright nastiness from those who should have been on their side, but eventually they had set up a number of schools which gave education and a hot meal at lunchtime to the poor. The number of young women wishing to help in this work grew. They became a religious community with a constitution and holy rule, both approved by Rome.

Anne, as their unofficial historian, had overcome her shyness enough to outline the growth of the order to an assembly of nuns.

Mother Eleanor was glad to see that all that expensive education had not gone entirely to waste. Of course, all the nuns had known the story of their founder, but they had not been confronted with facts and figures, not had to acknowledge how far some of their schools deviated from the original idea of providing education for poor girls who otherwise would have grown up illiterate and exploited. Mother Catherine had thought not only of these girls saving their immortal souls. She had also wanted them to be strong, spokeswomen of the church, inspiring, and leading. No wonder her bishop had tried to have her excommunicated.

Pauline had been so overcome by Anne's revelations that she proposed they sell all their properties and go and work in the slums of their cities as well as sending out missionaries to all the Third World countries. Reverend Mother saw no reason to disagree with the sentiments behind this plan but thought it should be discussed and thought about for a long time. Mother Church believed in hastening slowly. So slowly that the implementation of Pauline's ideas had still not found its way on to any agenda several years later.

Pauline kept for herself a large planning calendar on the wall of her room. Even then she sometimes found herself double booked, but moved at such lightning speed that she completed her duties ahead of schedule. Most evenings an hour of music helped her body and mind unwind.

Anne had no such outlet.

Eileen didn't run to a wall-planned day but she did fill a small diary at the beginning of each week from the numerous notes she had written to herself. This coming week was busy as Easter drew near. Her chaplaincy at the local hospital meant she called there once a week, usually taking communion to a few patients and stopping by the beds of others to talk awhile.

Mrs Cameron was getting very frail, and she tried to call on her at least three times a week. Karen needed to be prodded out of total inactivity, and Amber-Mae certainly needed her, poor little pet. The catechetical work in the parish was always with her, and, while she declined to also run the youth club, they seemed to need assistance from time to time. She wasn't quite sure why young people needed endless diversion to save them from a life of profligacy and apostasy, but did not confide in the parish priest about her doubts.

After Eileen's third attempt to contact her, Clare answered the phone.

'A bit like the pot calling the kettle black', said Eileen. 'Where have you been?'

'At the refuge, and then I had to do some shopping on the way home. I forgot to stock up on Friday. Did you get my message?'

'I did. What's the problem?'

Clare explained that one of the latest arrivals at the women's refuge was a Vietnamese woman who spoke little English. She had heard Eileen mention that one of her catechists spoke fluent Vietnamese. Clare wondered if she would help out with interpreting and moral support. Eileen promised to give the woman a call. She was about to hang up when Clare said: 'By the way, I met that little girl again, and her mother'.

'What little girl?' asked Eileen. There were numerous little girls in her life.

'Amber-Mae. The one you brought for Christmas dinner.'

Eileen felt fear. Had Karen and Amber-Mae fled to the refuge while she was spiritually enriching herself?

Clare went on. 'They came to our fete. Bought half the homemade-sweet stall. No wonder Karen is such a big girl. She said she might come to one of our confidence courses.'

'Saying and doing are two different things', replied Eileen. 'She said she might go to a cooking class and a typing class and a child-care class, and there was even some talk of china painting and, I think, pottery. She has trouble getting started. I'm sure any course would do her the world of good. She leads a pretty dreary life.'

Chapter Seven

Something about confidence must have caught Karen's fancy where the other topics had failed. She told Eileen she would like to start the next Thursday, except that the creche couldn't take Amber-Mae. Aaron was fine but they had no vacancies for three-year-olds.

Eileen called her bluff, and the following Thursday Amber-Mae was standing at the front door of the convent holding her doll and a little basket with some lollies and a banana.

'Mind you be good for Sister or I'll belt you one', threatened Karen, who then continued on her way pushing Aaron in his pram.

She really must be determined, thought Eileen, because she'll have to walk quite a few blocks and up a steep hill, and our Karen isn't overly fond of exercise. Good luck to her. She looked at Karen in a new light. Or was it Clare who had the knack of getting Karen out of the house and on the road to fulfilment?

Eileen rearranged her routine slightly and now did her Sunday school preparation on Thursday mornings, with Amber-Mae to help her. This meant that Amber-Mae coloured in the corner of a palm tree that would feature on Palm Sunday. She helped stack small palm leaves in a box ready to distribute to the children. She listened while Eileen told her about Jesus riding a donkey into the city with all the people cheering. She talked a lot about Aaron and her friend's cat, whose kittens had all gone away suddenly. Then she watched Playschool on television and spilt her milk on the carpet.

Karen arrived, quite excited about her course. She sat, Aaron on her lap and Amber-Mae trying to capture her attention with a drawing she had done, and told Eileen all about her morning. Much of it had been spent affirming good things about herself, and she felt quite cheered to discover how many there were. Eileen wondered, and then felt nasty inside at her doubts. God loves Karen, probably more than he loves me, she thought. Karen doesn't have uncharitable thoughts.

The house was peaceful when they left. Motherhood was a mixed blessing, Eileen reflected as she put the study back to order. Then she thought of Amber-Mae's excited little face absorbed in her colouring, and found herself feeling strangely lonely.

Clare had more problems. She called around later that evening, being in what she called a 'state'. 'Would you believe it? After all this time and with a young baby he gets religious scruples. The man's a nut case.'

'Who?' asked Eileen.

'Ted, of course. He had the effrontery to call around, with a bunch of flowers wilting in his puny hand, and say he had a proposition for me. He has decided that we are still married in the eyes of the church so he has no right to be living with Kimberley. "What about the baby?" I say. "Are you living in sin with the baby?" "That is unfortunate, and naturally I will see that the baby is properly cared for, although her mother is quite capable of earning a good living when the baby is a little older. I do not expect her to go back to work just yet", he replies. "Don't you care about Kimberley and your daughter?" I ask him. And he goes on with a lot of twaddle about religious beliefs and morality and how he sinned by leaving the church but he intends to make up for it. And then he asked if he could come back! Not to the house, not just yet, but if I would allow him to do up the old sleepout as a self-contained flat he could live there and work towards our reconciliation. He even asked if I forgave him for leaving me, when I was the one who asked him to move out. Of course the real reason is he can't afford to run three households, so if he is to assuage his religious scruples by leaving Kimberley and the baby and continue to pay maintenance for his three hulking teenagers he can't afford to also rent a flat. I got all of that out of him in the end. The reconciliation was an afterthought, after he had done his sums. I still can't get over his absolute cheek.'

Clare was so cross she couldn't see the funny side of it. Eileen made her coffee. Clare fumed on. 'Religion has got nothing to do with it. He just wants an out and this gives him the perfect excuse. Poor woman. I told you she'd end up wishing she'd never met Ted. He said he was considering the priesthood! They're not that desperate, are they?' She stirred her coffee vigorously.

'Are you going to let him have the sleepout?' Eileen asked.

'I thought about it. I thought it might be handy to have a baby-sitter on tap as I often get called out to the refuge at night and I don't like leaving the kids in the house on their own. I'm not interested in meeting any other man, so he wouldn't cramp my style. I also started to feel a bit sorry for him. Do you know what made me decide against it?'

'No', said Eileen.

'That friend of Mum whose husband lived in the back shed. Edith someone, and she never called her husband anything but 'him'.

There is no way I am going to have a miserable bent figure shuffling around under the clothes line waiting to be invited in to watch television.'

'Ted doesn't quite fit that picture', Eileen said, half laughing.

'Not yet. But he might get that way. If he has moral and money problems they are his problems and he can sort them out himself. He shouldn't have left in the first place if he wasn't sure about what he was doing. Oh, Eileen, what a mess. I feel angry and ashamed and exasperated all in one. I do envy you your peaceful life. For goodness sake don't tell Mum, because she'll think it is the answer to her prayers.'

Ted and Clare's separation had certainly been traumatic for her parents. They had seemed the perfect Catholic family, even having the parish priest around for dinner every Sunday night. Clare used to joke about Ted and his harem, because he was the chairman to eight spinster ladies on the parish council. Clare founded the Liturgy Group, which used to arrange home masses once a month for the more progressive members of the congregation and folksy hymns for the Sunday parish masses. The harem gave the home masses a miss, and tried to avoid the noisier Sunday masses by attending at 8 am, when the atmosphere was more prayerful.

Clare had loved those home masses, where they were all so involved. Four couples formed the regular group, with visitors from time to time. Mostly the readings came from Scripture, but sometimes one of them would choose a poem or spiritual reading which they felt was apt and inspiring. Prayers of the faithful, when they voiced their petitions, were heartfelt. Truly the Lord was present in Clare's lounge room on those evenings.

Ted complained that they were too casual. You shouldn't re-enact Calvary sitting on the floor using the coffee-table as an altar. He acknowledged that they were following in the steps of the early Christians, but a lot of paths had been trodden since then. You couldn't wipe out nearly two thousand years of tradition on a whim. Ted had never felt uncomfortable in the anonymity of the Latin mass, and he missed the plainsong.

The parish council could cope with the idea of home masses. But they had been outraged when the Liturgy Group had organised a Mass for Peace during the Vietnam Moratorium protests. They recognised the danger of harbouring a group which was tainted with communism. Vatican Council had said nothing about consorting with the enemy. Ted gave his support, somewhat reluctantly, to Clare.

The parish priest vacillated. On the one hand, he did not want to lose his chairman. On the other, he did not want to offend his spinster ladies (one of whom had the ear of the bishop), who were the backbone of the parish administration. The poor man suffered agonies of indecision, until Ted took the initiative and resigned.

After a week of deep thinking, Ted shook the dust of the church from his shoes. He could no longer see the Holy Ghost's guidance in the church, and doubted the existence of any such being. Without the blessed Trinity the whole Catholic doctrine became untenable. Thank God he had seen the light. He entered atheism with the fervour of any convert.

The children asked why he no longer went to mass. They couldn't see why they had to go when Daddy didn't. The house became quarrelsome.

Clare started to go to daily mass, but not to her parish church. The priest who said their home masses left the priesthood and married an ex-nun. Clare felt that they had shaken free from the barriers of orthodox and unthinking obedience and yet had not reached the promised land. Less and less she felt the need to pray, and only went to mass each Sunday out of stubbornness.

Until she met Brenda.

Brenda, she said, changed her life. Brenda freed her from the stultifying middle-class sexist crap she had been subjected to all her life. Brenda opened her eyes to the way she had been used and abused, placed in a pigeonhole. She loaned her books.

Clare went to feminist discussion groups and became a new, confident, affirming person.

Ted did not like the new Clare very much. He blamed her upbringing, which he felt had not been strict enough. Freed from the external restraints imposed by society and the church, she was losing all sense of restraint and decorum. She dressed like a plumber. He was certainly not sexist, but he preferred a woman who had some feminine graces. Clare suggested that, if he wasn't happy in her company, he could always leave and she would consult a lawyer.

Ted did leave. Their divorce and property settlement was no more acrimonious than most, and the children stayed with Clare.

Clare's mother was devastated. She found it very hard to forgive Ted for deserting his wife and children, although she knew she must, or never say the Lord's Prayer again.

Holy Week was upon them. Unlike most of the population, Eileen, Anne, and Pauline did not think of Easter as an extra long weekend. To them it was the most joyous feast in the church's year.

Anne worked hard during the early part of the week to finally complete her thesis. This entailed a thorough audit of her references, final proofread, and rewriting of one or two paragraphs. Anne being who she was, the thesis would be painstakingly presented, have reliably explored and expounded the current thinking on medieval mysticism, have very little original to say, and would result in Anne being a PhD. Eileen realised that it was not always the most brilliant scholars who reaped the academic honours. Plodders had their place. She and Pauline also hoped that, with the thesis out of the way, Anne would finally reach her decision. A difficult decision made agonising by procrastination. The situation made the whole house jumpy.

Pauline was busy organising liturgical celebrations at school. 'Not so easy', she complained, 'when we aren't there for the main events. I encourage them all to attend the services at their parish churches, but I suspect half the senior girls are going camping with their boyfriends and won't go near a church.'

Anne was shocked. She had little to do with the real world.

If she does leave, thought Eileen, she will be in for a few more shocks. Unless she takes up the life of a hermit and retreats from the world altogether.

Pauline was very proud of the stations of the cross which the year eleven students had prepared during the term, and which were now positioned in the school courtyard and corridor. Some antisocial child had written 'Rolling Stones rule' on the fifth station in red paint, causing a witch-hunt which reverberated throughout the entire school. The culprit, finally dobbed in by her panicking friends, sobbingly apologised in front of the whole school at an assembly, and almost renounced the Rolling Stones in the process. Pauline could see the funny side of it, but she was genuinely upset by the incident. She wondered how effective her religious education program really was.

Eileen had different problems with her Sunday school. She contended that to teach religion you really needed a diploma in art. On Palm Sunday the back wall of the church was decorated with a huge mural depicting Christ's triumphant entry into Jerusalem. She had drawn the main figures, and her enthusiastic pupils had filled in the shapes. Where their colouring in went over the line, she managed to arrange a palm leaf so that no-one would ever know. The children had drawn their faces on the people in the crowd. If self-portraits were good enough for Leonardo and Michelangelo, why not for Deborah, Mark, Jeanette, and the others? Not even their parents would recognise them, but it made the events of so long ago relevant to her children. The little ones reacted with great enthusiasm, but it was harder to reach the older children.

'At least it looks as if we are doing something on Sunday mornings', she said to Anne. 'It's not so different from those medieval churches which had the Bible stories depicted on the walls, in the stained-glass windows, or in the wood and bronze carvings.'

Anne wondered if she had left something out of her thesis which was vital. She had never considered the role of art in the medieval church. Did it relate to mysticism? The thought of adding as much as one more comma exhausted her. That could be a topic for one of her students to cover. She seemed to spend a lot of time coming and going, carrying cardboard boxes out of the house and returning empty-handed. Pauline wondered if she had to deliver her references with her thesis. Anne would have used half the library before putting finger to typewriter key.

On Holy Thursday night they all attended the evening ceremonies. Eileen was tired of being indignant that only men were welcomed at the altar to have their feet washed. They must be the cleanest feet in the church, she thought, even before the priest's token sprinkle in remembrance of Christ washing his apostles' feet. Maybe it was historically correct to have only men, but they didn't strictly adhere to history in every part of the ceremonies. More evidence of women's second-class citizenship. Was it a member of the Curia who first said 'hasten slowly'?

The blessed sacrament was to be left on the Altar of Repose throughout the night while the people took turns to pray. Jesus often went up into the mountains and prayed all night. She discussed it with Pauline, and they both agreed that if they prayed all night they would be useless in the morning. Yet Jesus managed to continue his work of preaching and healing. Perhaps he was a night person. Eileen knew that she was a morning person.

She needed her time of prayer, meditation, and yoga early each day. It was a spiritual charge to her battery, but it hardly rated against an all-night vigil. Kneeling in the dimly lit church, she tried to keep her mind on her prayers. Praying was the key to spiritual success, but it was not always easy. It could become a list of requests.

At the old convent people would ring and ask for prayers for all sorts of needs. They might have a close relative who was desperately ill, an examination, or a job interview. The request was put on the noticeboard. Nuns preferred to choose a particular intention to concentrate on, rather than pray for people in general. To pray for particular people kept them in touch with the outside world to a far greater extent than laypeople realised.

Nuns also prayed for their families. They prayed for their own souls, for patience, perseverance, humility, and help against temptation. On this particular night Eileen prayed that her parents would continue to be healthy and together. She knew either would be very lonely if the other died. She prayed for Clare, who she sensed was not at peace. Too much frenetic activity and bad language. A tiredness around her eyes, none of her old bounce. Clare worked hard and helped women, but who was there to help her? She thought, then, of Karen and Amber-Mae. Her prayers centred on the young child, who had little chance to grow up as anything but a second Karen. She knew God would understand that was not meant to be an uncharitable thought, just a realistic one. She prayed then for Anne, that she would make the right decision, whatever that decision might be. She prayed for world peace and the suffering people of the Third World. She wondered if she should volunteer for missionary work. She had always wanted to travel. It had been one of the sorrows of her life that she had never had the chance to see the great art treasures in Europe, never visited Milan and seen Leonardo's *Last Supper* or the *Pieta* of Michelangelo. Was that a selfish desire? She believed that such an experience would bring her closer to God. Wasn't that why God made us creative beings?

Eileen, she thought, your mind is wandering. She said the Lord's Prayer very slowly to discipline her thoughts. Then she thought about their recent retreat. For each it had had a different message. Nothing she did was spectacularly successful, but if she was faithful in small things she was pleasing God. Maybe volunteering for overseas mission work or Australian Volunteers Abroad was being a bit flashy.

Her hour up, she stayed a little longer. It was good to be there. The church was quiet and restful, unlike the Sunday masses, when it was all bustle, singing, and activity. People came into the church then talking among themselves. There was a lack of reverence, which she found distressing. Surely they could contain themselves for an hour? Was anything so important that it had to be talked about when they should be praying to God? She remembered how her mother would tap her firmly on the shoulder if she so much as thought about talking to Clare in church. Her mother always knew. Clare, who had seemed so secure in her faith now danced to a different tune. She'd found a domestic Volunteers Abroad in her neighbourhood. Eileen would say that God worked in mysterious ways. Clare would say she hadn't noticed God at any of the committee meetings.

Eileen accepted her distracting thoughts as a sign that it was time she went home to bed.

The three nuns fasted until after the ceremony on Good Friday, which they attended at the cathedral, where the music was inspirational. You had to have something to take your mind off your aching back, sore knees, and rumbling tummy, according to Pauline, and Good Friday was not a day to be too wimpish about ailments.

Eileen had read the gospel passages about the crucifixion for her morning meditation. Sister Josephine told them that Christ had chosen such an agonising death to prove how much he loved each one of us. 'He would have died for just one person', Sister had said, 'so when you sin you are adding to the sorrow he felt on the cross'.

The fact that Jesus would have died just for her, if she had been the only person who had ever lived, made an enormous impression on Eileen. You couldn't ignore love like that, but she had always wanted to tell Jesus that he didn't have to die so painfully. It made her feel the necessity to do something in return. Was that what had led the saints to a life of extreme penance?

She used her method of imagining herself there, standing at the foot of the cross with the other women. The men, she noted, had all fled in terror. The women stood by faithfully. Always on Good Friday she had felt a great sense of relief when it was three o'clock and Jesus' sufferings were over.

Pauline had made hot cross buns of which she was inordinately proud. They ate them for afternoon tea when they returned from the cathedral, and only ate a small vegetarian meal that evening. Anne would scarcely have noticed the difference from a normal day, but Pauline, having the hearty appetite of an active person, went to bed with an empty feeling in her stomach.

Holy Saturday evening. Joy, light, candles, baptismal water, ancient rites. The church celebrating the event which justified her faith. Death, where is thy sting?

There was a happy buzz as the congregation, wishing each other a happy Easter, left the cathedral porch. The mild day had become a chill night, and people pulled their coats around themselves as they hurried to their cars. The traffic was heavy as they joined the revellers who had been at parties celebrating the long weekend. Pauline drove carefully, saying she didn't want to become a statistic before she had eaten her Easter egg.

Eileen still felt tired as she walked along the street, now full of sunshine, to the parish church for Easter Sunday. If the Palm Sunday display had been eye-catching, the Easter Sunday display which her children had been preparing for most of Lent was arresting. A purist might even have called their array of colourful posters and decorated candles gaudy. Easter was an alive time, and you can't express that in muted colours. The parish mass lacked the grandeur of the vigil service at the cathedral. Poor old Jennifer did her best on the wheezy organ, and the congregation sang a bracket of hymns which seemed to have been originally composed for a hurdy-gurdy. Father Tom's sermon excelled in brevity. By the end of the Easter ceremonies his larynx was feeling the strain. Normally his great desire to gather them up into one big happy Christian family resulted in a long sermon and chatty asides all the way through mass.

Their Easter dinner was a continuation of the celebration. Anne had completed and submitted her thesis. She looked ten years younger. Pauline had finished all the corrections she had brought home from school, leaving Monday as a free day. Eileen's efforts in the kitchen had been more successful than usual, and the others genuinely complimented her on her roast lamb and apple crumble.

Pauline and Eileen washed the dishes, Eileen reminiscing about the way she and Clare used to sing when they washed up.

'What sort of songs?' asked Pauline.

'Old Irish ones usually', replied Eileen, and she and Pauline launched forth tunefully into 'When Irish Eyes are Smiling'. They were singing with such gusto that they did not hear the front door close, although it closed so quietly they might not have heard it anyway.

Kitchen clean, Eileen knocked on Anne's door to invite her to come to the sitting room for a cup of tea and to talk. It was a bedroom, not a cell as they had called their rooms in the old convent. They were three rather than a hundred and three, but Eileen had felt very alive to them being a community over the Easter time. Christ had had only twelve apostles, but from those a great church had grown. They, too, could be effective in the outside world even though small in numbers.

Anne did not answer.

Eileen knocked again. Still no reply, so she gently opened the door to see if Anne was asleep,

The room was empty. No Anne, no books, the wardrobe door slightly ajar to reveal a black space. Only an envelope on the chest of drawers addressed to her and Pauline. Eileen picked it up but felt too nervous to open it. She carried it out to Pauline and handed it over as though it were a ticking time bomb. Pauline ripped it open, read for a few seconds, and then said: 'Well, she's left us. Couldn't face telling us, but this Adrian character has set her up in a flat near the university. She hopes we visit her sometime.'

Eileen sat down suddenly. Pauline handed her the letter, which she read for herself, although the words seemed to run all over the page.

'What do you mean "set her up"? Makes her sound like a fallen woman. All he has done is leased an apartment to her. She didn't find it too hard to tell *him* about it.'

Eileen felt desperately hurt. She could understand Anne leaving. Lots of the other nuns had, many quite soon after Vatican II and others in the years following, either because the changes went too far or because they did not go far enough. They wouldn't have blamed Anne. But going off so furtively, while she and Pauline were doing the dishes. After they had been together for so many years. Had done their novitiate together, studied together, changed from wearing their habits to normal clothes on the same day. Eileen didn't really like Anne as a person — that didn't matter. Theirs had been a closer bond than mere liking.

She and Pauline talked about it late into the night. Pauline was more matter-of-fact. They had to realise that Anne was a bit neurotic, possibly menopausal. 'Does funny things to some women. Hormones get all upset. It's easy to make jokes about it, but it can disrupt a woman's life drastically. We'll have to visit her soon and help her settle in.'

'I don't think she wants to see us', replied Eileen. 'I'm not sure I want to see her either.'

'Anne would have found trying to explain herself to us absolutely excruciating. We have to let her know we understand, and support her. It's a big step she's taken. I hope she has told the provincial. Should we write a letter, just in case?'

'Saying what?' asked Eileen.

Eileen fought with her sense of anger at Anne's desertion. She was in grief and needed time to feel herself again. They had been three, now they were only two.

'Explaining. She's a fugitive from religion at the moment and doomed to excommunication.'

'Don't be silly. It's not the Middle Ages. You write. I wouldn't know what to say.'

The next day Eileen woke feeling awful, and then she remembered that Anne had left. No point letting it make her feel depressed. Pauline had obviously come to the same conclusion as she bounced into the kitchen ready for breakfast. She sang a defiant song as she watched the toast, and then turned to Eileen.

'Just you and I now. Do you think that the provincial will send any of the other sisters to join us?'

'She might say we can't be trusted.' Eileen insisted on taking Anne's leaving as her responsibility.

'Do you think Anne has done the right thing?' Pauline asked.

'I hope so, for her sake', Eileen snapped, then apologised. If she kept this up, Pauline would be packing her bags too.

Monday was a bright, sunny day. Pauline was going bushwalking with an old school friend. Eileen thought she would go to see her mother and father. She wanted to sit in the old family home and be fussed over by her mother while she talked politics with her father. He had very definite views. No thaw in the Cold War would lead him to relax his vigilance. Her mother smiled indulgently as she poured the tea and sliced the sponge cake. She seemed weary. A week spent making Easter eggs for Clare to take to the women's refuge, plus all the praying in church, had quite worn her out, she said. And her garden was getting desperate. Eileen noticed the odd weed among the immaculate flowerbeds and reflected that her mother and Mrs Cameron were kindred spirits.

Clare had said that Christmas and Easter were busy times because they were drinking times. Eileen had come across some bad situations in her visits around the parish and to the hospital, but Clare seemed to have the monopoly on grisly stories. She spared her mother the grosser details, but her mother still felt saddened for these women who had lived in fear. Since she was practical, her pity took the form of sewing clothes, making rag dolls, and cooking nourishing soup. She also prayed, but she didn't tell Clare about that. Clare tended to become testy at the mention of spiritual matters.

'It shows she is not at ease with her conscience', said her mother to Eileen. 'She can't convince me that she has really lost her faith. She was such a staunch Catholic once. I do blame Ted for a lot of it. She must have found it hard when Ted deserted the church and then deserted his family.'

Eileen refrained from mentioning that Ted now wanted to return to his family. Clare would never forgive her if she betrayed her confidence. She suspected they had not heard the end of the Ted saga.

With her thoughts on Clare, Eileen decided to call at her house on her way home. No need to worry about the garden being desperate there. Clare had given up the struggle long ago and allowed plants to wander at will. Nagging occasionally induced one of the boys to mow the lawn, although threats of withheld pocket money were more effective. Elizabeth became an enthusiastic weeder depending on the state of her crush on the boy next door. Their relationship waned more than it waxed.

Clare, too, looked tired. It wasn't overwork or too much praying; it was Ted.

'He keeps coming around. He says it's to see the children, so I can't really stop him. The boys seem quite keen. I tried going out the nights he came around, but it got to be a bit ridiculous skulking around town waiting for my ex-husband to leave so I could go home to bed. I decided to go to my room and read or catch up on some of the refuge paperwork. You have no idea what the government expects us to go through to get our miserly grant. But I'm not sure the bedroom is such a great idea. Ted comes in to say goodnight, and he is getting a definite gleam in his eye. Stupid man!'

Clare sounded more exasperated than angry.

They had a sisterly evening, laughing and joking about their youthful exploits. Eileen was the older sister, but Clare was the one who had masterminded all the mischief.

Eileen returned to the suburban convent to find Pauline attending to a blister which had attempted, without success, to spoil her day. They prayed together before retiring. They prayed for the world and for their special intentions. They gave thanks for the day of rest and recreation. They prayed for Anne.

Anne would have been grateful for all the prayers, had she known. She paced about her lonely flat, tried to watch television but gave up, disgusted by the sheer mindlessness of it all. She wanted to ring Eileen but didn't know what to say. She wanted to kneel down with Eileen and Pauline and say her evening prayers, have a cup of cocoa, and go to bed in her old room. There were strange noises outside. What if someone broke in? She had not been alone in a house in all her adult life before this. Her body ached with tension, loneliness, and fear. She couldn't pray. She wasn't sure if God would listen to her. Maybe he was too disappointed in her for leaving. She read for a bit, cried a little, thought about having a bath but decided against it in case a burglar broke in while she was naked. Finally she fell asleep.

Next morning, packing up her papers for university and drinking a morning cup of tea in the sunny corner of the kitchen, she laughed at her fears. Evening was hours away.

Karen had a new hairstyle. One week of assertiveness training and she had gone 'burnished copper'. With a swing in her step she walked up the path with Amber-Mae trotting alongside. Aaron was asleep in his pram.

'Let's hope he stays that way', said Karen. 'He was a proper little pest last week. Mind you be good for Sister.'

'Amber-Mae is always good, aren't you, pet?' replied Eileen, but Karen was halfway up the path, hurrying to self-fulfilment.

'I see you had your little friend today', commented Pauline.

'Yes. Thursday's our day', Eileen replied

'She left some graffiti in the toilet.'

Amber-Mae had drawn a misshapen cat on the wall in biro. Eileen scrubbed at it but only succeeded in turning it into a furry misshapen cat.

The following Thursday Karen arrived announcing she had lost two kilograms, and she would give up smoking but she was scared she would put on weight. Eileen encouraged her. She planned to take Amber-Mae to visit Mrs Cameron. It would do the old lady good to have a little girl around.

Mrs Cameron clucked and fussed and helped Amber-Mae make a gingerbread man with sultana eyes and a cherry mouth. Minnie sulked. Eileen cleaned the bathroom while Mrs Cameron was distracted. Mrs Cameron gave Amber-Mae some tartan ribbon, and Eileen plaited her hair and tied it with two bows. Amber-Mae twirled around when her mother called to collect her, but Karen didn't notice. She was too full of her communication exercise. She had role-played a single mother demanding her rights from a Social Service Department person who had lost her file. The others in the class had said she was great at acting. She was thinking of doing an acting course when this course finished. 'You never know', she said. Eileen felt she did know. Copper hair and a few kilos lost did not turn Karen into screen material.

She suspected that Pauline had contacted Anne but didn't ask. They moved warily with each other, allowing the three to become a comfortable two.

Pauline blamed herself for becoming lax. 'I have an electric blanket on my bed. No wonder Anne left.'

Eileen saw the connection, but she comforted Pauline. 'St Thérèse used to warm her hands and feet at the fire before she went to her cell at night.'

'Hardly the same thing. She lived in a draughty French convent in the middle of winter. She probably had to warm her feet to find out if they were still there. We have to pray together more. Which mass are you going to on Sunday?'

Pauline never went to the same Sunday mass as Eileen because there were too many children there. She had her fill of them during the week and preferred the earlier quieter mass. Eileen did too, but was trapped by the Sunday school, children's liturgy, and guitars. The Easter services at the cathedral had been a treat.

Chapter Eight

Eileen lay on her back on the floor, legs uncrossed, hands by her side, palms facing the ceiling. She breathed in through the soles of her feet. She breathed in spiritual awareness, breathed out love of self. Breathed in love for Anne, breathed out anger and hurt. Breathed in understanding for Karen, breathed out exasperation. Breathed in strength, breathed out weakness. Breathed in peace and tranquillity, breathed out anxiety and tension. With her eyes closed she concentrated her energies on love of God and love for people. Then she stood up, stretched every part of her body, and knelt down to complete her morning prayers.

She always knelt, a habit from childhood. She had tried praying in the lotus position but her knees felt uncomfortable and distracted her. How the yogis sat in that position for hours eluded her. Western knees were for kneeling. She meditated on the words of the Magnificat. 'My soul doth magnify the Lord, and my Spirit hath rejoiced in God my Saviour.' She always used this translation. Modern versions robbed it of poetry for her, and, like a mantra, she needed to run the words through and through her mind, or chant them softly. No wonder she liked to say her morning prayers alone. Pauline would wonder what on earth she was doing.

Eileen surmised that Pauline's prayers consisted of the morning offering, acts of faith, hope, and charity, and a decade of the rosary. Guilt! How dare she be so smug! What right had she to judge Pauline's spiritual progress, and who was she to say that standing on her head was more efficacious to the soul than a decade of the rosary. All the nice feeling from her meditation evaporated in a second.

Pauline had made toast and boiled the kettle for her instant coffee and Eileen's herbal tea. Her basket of corrected books stood at the door ready for her flight to school.

'I was thinking', she said. 'Anne's bedroom is not being used. I could set it up as a study.'

'A great idea', replied Eileen. 'I could do with a room to prepare the Sunday school material and the catechists worksheets, and keep a file on all the parish visitations. Father Tom will be most impressed by my efficiency.'

'I was thinking of using it for my school work. I'm always bringing stacks of stuff home and my bedroom gets very messy-looking.'

'You have a study desk at school.'

'You could use a room at the parish house.'

Eileen frowned at her cup of tea. Neither of them spoke for a long minute. Then they spoke together.

'You have it.'

They laughed.

'Why can't we set it up for both?' said Eileen. 'You can have a desk in one corner and I'll have a table in the other, and we can put in a filing cabinet and bookcase. We could even get one of those winding cords for the phone and make it a real office. I'll use it during the day and you can have it at night.'

'And one poster each on the wall', added Pauline, knowing Eileen's penchant for colourful inspiring messages.

'We can put the other furniture in the garage in case we need it again.'

They both thought of Anne.

Mother Provincial's reply to Pauline's letter telling her about Anne's departure had been barely charitable. Anne had been 'a treasure in the community', 'an academic whose reputation brought them all into good repute'. She didn't quite ask how they had let this prize slip through their fingers but she did remind them that charity and community love should have foreseen and forestalled. She would write to Anne herself.

How would Anne react to being the order's prize show pony? Eileen wondered. No doubt with gratification, but now she was more intent on becoming the theology department's show pony. Mother Provincial's good opinion was as naught next to that of Adrian and Christine. Or was it just Adrian? Eileen dismissed that thought as being unworthy. So much for meditation in the morning. She had hardly finished her breakfast and she was sinning against charity. How did the saints do it?

Clare came to see her that night, auburn hair wild around her face, hands clenched and unclenched as she talked about this and that: the refuge, the children, the course she was going to run on Women's Legal Rights, and Karen. She was delighted with the change in Karen, who seemed to be taking a responsible attitude towards self-improvement.

'She's finally prepared to own her problems instead of blaming everybody else. That's always an important step.'

Eileen, who had known Karen for several months, felt less hopeful. She doubted her staying power.

'Women like Karen puzzle me. They don't seem to have any purpose in life, and they justify their existence by getting pregnant even though they don't really want a child. At least Karen has her baby instead of getting rid of it, poor little thing', said Eileen somewhat primly.

'You think all abortion is wrong?' asked Clare. 'Of course you would.'

'Don't you?' asked Eileen, surprised.

'Not since I started working at the women's refuge. That can change your mind about a lot of things.'

'Some things are unchangeable. To me abortion is taking the life of an innocent person.'

'It's not that simple. Anyway, it's not a situation you'll ever have to worry about. You can be thankful for that', replied Clare, who was too tired to start an argument.

Just before she left she admitted to having something she needed to talk about, but not that night. She forgot herself enough to say 'Pray for me' as she hurried out the door.

Eileen did pray for her. She remembered her in her daily mass and worried about her as she went from task to task.

Mrs Cameron didn't seem able to shake off her nasty cough. The chemist had sold her an elixir which smelt like licorice and tasted vile. Mrs Cameron swallowed it down following it with hot water as instructed but felt little better. Her daughter was looking into homes and private hospitals for the aged. Mrs Cameron did not want to go.

'And what about Minnie? They won't have her in a home. I want to stay here where I've always lived. I'm too old to learn new ways.'

The hospital visitation took Eileen more time than usual. The patients all seemed to need to talk to someone. Half the world's problems could be solved if the other half was prepared to listen, Eileen thought.

She intended ringing Clare that night, but she had to go to a catechists meeting and didn't get home until late. The next night she had a parish council meeting, and on the Wednesday she went to the school play with Pauline. On Thursday Karen mentioned that Clare had not seemed too well, and Eileen, feeling guilty, did ring only to find that Clare was not home.

'Just tell her I rang', she asked Elizabeth, who had shown complete surprise to hear that her mother had not been well. Perhaps Karen had imagined it. No imagination about Karen losing weight, keeping her hair well groomed, and being star of the sewing class.

'Size fourteen now, and I'll keep going until I'm size twelve. Size fourteen's OK, but. Fergie wears fourteen and she looks all right to me.'

Eileen had gleaned from Mrs Cameron that Fergie was now size twelve and taking motherhood seriously, but she didn't burden Karen with that information. Mrs Cameron had little time for any of the royal family except the queen and queen mother.

How would Sister Josephine have coped with the young royals? she wondered. How would Sister Josephine have coped with the eighties?

The next time Eileen heard from Clare she was in hospital. The matron rang at about 10pm and Eileen left straightaway, driving too fast through the almost deserted streets. Arriving at the hospital, she rushed into the lift and pressed the button for the fourth floor. Matron was at her desk.

'She's all right now, just a bit tired. It was a minor complication. Not usual in such an early T.O.P. The doctor gave her an injection and the bleeding has stopped. It's the third door down on your left. If she is asleep don't wake her.'

The significance of what matron had said only hit her halfway down the corridor. T.O.P. Termination of pregnancy.

Clare had a room to herself. Her eyes were closed, her face almost as pale as the pillowslip. She must have heard Eileen enter, because she opened her eyes, smiled, and held out her hand.

'Thanks for coming. I feel much better now. It was frightening for a while. I felt as though I was floating away and nothing could stop me. I wouldn't let them ring Ted. Whatever you do, don't tell Mum.'

She closed her eyes again.

Eileen sat, holding her hand, feeling guilty. If only she had been more sympathetic before, more approachable, instead of the prim theologian. No wonder Clare couldn't confide in her. And now her baby was dead. Was it a boy or a girl? How could Clare have not wanted to have her baby?

Eileen sat very still. She couldn't pray. Not properly. She mingled her thoughts with a being she called God and experienced thoughts and emotions too tangled to be verbalised. She knew that God understood.

Matron tiptoed in and beckoned her. 'There's not much point your staying unless you really want to. The doctor gave her something to help her sleep. Come back tomorrow. She's in no danger.'

The matron was an old friend, who had the sensitivity to say nothing more than, 'Goodnight. God bless.'

Eileen drove straight home and went to bed, but could not sleep. Her mind was disturbed. The younger sister, whose achievements she had admired and whose exploits she had tried to curb. Headstrong and determined, Clare never did things by halves. If only Clare had confided in her she would have helped her. The baby needn't have been destroyed. She, Eileen, could have helped to look after it. A boy or girl? she wondered again. Clare helped so many other women who were in trouble but had no-one to help her. Eileen knew that she had failed when she was needed.

The next day Clare told her the rest of the story. A birthday dinner that Ted and the children had arranged for her as a surprise. Ted growing amorous over coffee and mints. Clare growing mellow after a few glasses of champagne. They had finished the night in their matrimonial bed. 'I didn't even enjoy it all that much', Clare complained. I must admit that my experience is limited, but I don't think that Ted is one of the great lovers of this world. I was furious when I realised that I was pregnant. I wouldn't believe it at first. Tried to convince myself it was premature menopause. You can imagine how I felt.'

Eileen couldn't.

'Didn't tell Ted. No way! Imagine how he would have reacted! I was feeling too sick to cope with that. I nearly told you, but then I decided that it wasn't fair to burden you with my problems. I know you can't approve of what I did, but I really couldn't have faced another child. I just couldn't.' Her voice rose. She stopped talking, pausing to gain control. 'Having children isn't all bliss, you know. I envy you sometimes. The only person you really have to worry about is yourself.'

'That makes me sound rather selfish.' Eileen felt surprised to hear her life thus described. She longed to tell Clare how much she would have loved to have had a child. How she would have taken Clare's little unwanted baby, cherished and cared for her. Or him. But the habit of not talking about oneself is hard to break.

'If you really envy me, come and join me for a while. We have a spare room now.'

'Oh Eileen, don't tempt me. I could do with a week of peace and quiet and time to think. I've never fathomed out what you do all day, although I know you are busy. At least, you never seem to be there to answer the phone. Just to have time to sit and think. What a luxury.'

Eileen told Clare she should spend a week just following her around and see how rested she felt at the end. There was certainly no time for champagne dinners on her birthday. At times her life seemed to be a series of meetings strung together by visits to the hospital and to those in the parish who needed pastoral care, with a Sunday school lesson for light relief.

'You don't approve, do you?' Clare asked her. 'Let's be frank with each other just this once.'

'It's not for me to judge. I mean that sincerely. But, Clare, I wish you had spoken to me before. Maybe I could have helped you.'

'Would you have come with me to the hospital and held my hand during the surgery?' Clare defied Eileen but was near tears.

'If it was what you wanted I would have been there. You are my sister.'

Clare did cry then. Eileen moved next to her and put her arm around her shoulders.

'It doesn't matter, Clare. It's all over now. Don't cry.'

She was the big sister once more. As she hugged Clare, Eileen had the spiritual arrogance to pray to God that Clare would feel no guilt. 'Let me take her guilt unto myself', she prayed. 'Let her suffering be mine as she is my sister.'

Clare stayed in hospital for one more day. As far as the rest of the family knew, she had needed exploratory surgery, but was being released with a clean bill of health. Her mother thanked God for Clare's good fortune. Ted fussed a lot and said she needed looking after, the implication being that he was the one to do it. Her children washed up the evening dishes without argument for a few nights, and then settled back to normal practice.

Invited for Sunday tea at the convent the following weekend, Clare seemed quite cheerful, laughing and joking with Pauline, who had returned home from supervising the cross-country team on one of its inevitable failure missions.

'We've got two good runners, only one of whom trains. The other girls in the team are there for the chance to meet the boys who are competing from other schools. If they put as much energy into running as into arranging their hair, we might even stand a chance in the inter-school championships', Pauline said.

Clare entertained them with some of the more spectacular stories from the women's refuge, which was constantly under siege from avenging husbands. It seemed funny in retrospect, but she never became used to seeing little children crouching in terror as their fathers roared threats or thumped on the door. Their better natures assumed ascendancy at the sound of the police-car siren. As Clare left she announced breezily that she would take Eileen up on her offer for the spare room quite soon.

Pauline was horrified. 'That's our study, not the spare room. I thought we had settled that. One of the teachers from school was hinting about staying here but I put her off.'

'I don't think Clare means it. She's just in love with the idea of our tranquil lives', Eileen reassured. 'She thinks we only worry about ourselves.'

Pauline didn't bother making the obvious response. There were more exciting things to discuss. She had seen Anne that morning, who had invited them around one evening next week.

'She suggested Friday. Does that suit you?'

Eileen looked at her diary. 'I'm free after six. There's a meeting of the first communicants and their families at four-thirty. I miss the old first communions, with the children dressed in white and the big communion breakfast afterwards. All those lovely sentimental hymns and the mums crying all over the church. I know the family's more involved now, but the spectacle has gone. The church has lost a lot of colour.'

'Do you want to go?' asked Pauline, refusing to be diverted.

'To Anne's? Why not? It will be nice to see her again.'

Eileen came down with a cold — sniffle-snuffling misery. She was determined to be better before Friday, which was four days away. Pauline offered herbal remedies, Vicks, garlic tablets, and her hot-water bottle, none of which made her feel a great deal better. Eileen felt lethargic and depressed, unusual for her. The early morning prayer and meditation failed to relax her. In fact, she felt added tension from trying to force herself to relax. The dreams came later, but before that she was aware of an uneasiness, a heaviness. Pauline said she looked awful, but most people do with a cold.

Karen noticed she was looking peaky and offered to take Amber-Mae to her sewing class.

'If you are worried about her catching my cold it might be a good idea', said Eileen, 'but I think I'm over the worst of it now. The germs are giving up.'

Amber-Mae started to cry. 'I want to stay with Sister Eileen', she sobbed, bouncing up and down in frustration. Karen pulled a face as if to say What can you do? and set off up the path pushing Aaron, whose bellows were now mingling with his sister's cries. Amber-Mae stopped as soon as she sensed victory was hers, took Eileen's hand, and headed down the passage.

'Would you like to come and visit Mrs Cameron?' Eileen asked. 'The lady with the dog. I think she has a cold too.' Amber-Mae loved driving in the car, so she gave her consent to the proposal.

Mrs Cameron's cold was the persistent type, and she was sitting up in bed, a shawl wrapped around her shoulders, listening to the radio when they got there. Eileen knew she was feeling poorly, because Minnie was sitting on the end of the bed. Mrs Cameron, scrupulously clean, did not usually allow the dog on her bed. The bedroom carpet was her limit.

'I can't understand why some of these people ring in. They talk such utter nonsense', she complained. 'Either that or they are whingeing about something. Life doesn't get any better for complaining about it.'

'How are you feeling?' Eileen asked.

'On the mend, except for the cough. I'm not going into a home, not for all the daughters in the world. She's keeping at me, you know, but I won't give in. Besides, there's Minnie.'

Eileen's reply was drowned by a crash and a wail. Amber-Mae appeared at the door of the bedroom holding a piece of vase in her hand. Her eyes were filled with tears. 'It broke. I dropped it.'

Mrs Cameron tried hard to hide her disappointment. 'Not the red vase? It was a wedding present. You shouldn't have touched it. Oh well, it was an accident I suppose. Don't cry, little girl. Would you like a barley sugar? Here.'

A bony hand holding a white bag emerged from the shawl. Amber-Mae inched forward and reached out. Eileen noted the clear, soft flesh on her arm. Mrs Cameron's arm must have looked like that once.

Chapter Nine

The light from Anne's flat shone down the front path. It was a two-storey unit flanked by high fences and shrubs to create an illusion of privacy. Anne said the neighbours were generally quiet anyway, and she had only spoken to the one on the left briefly about garbage collection. It was a neighbourhood where people kept to themselves.

Eileen and Pauline were all curiosity as Anne greeted them. This was the promised land to which she had fled looking for a fulfilment denied her in their convent. Whoever had furnished the flat (it was Adrian) had questionable taste and an adequate bank account. Here was Anne, devotee of medieval mysticism, with a crystal mini-chandelier in the lounge-room and a dishwasher in the kitchen. Worse, the bathroom contained a spa. Wonderful for releasing tension, she told them, and offered them a go. Pauline was tempted, but, seeing the expression on Eileen's face, decided against it. The main feature of the bedroom was not the frilled double bed but the coat stand, on which hung a cashmere coat. Eileen had always wanted a cashmere coat. At least, if she had been worldly instead of vowed to poverty, she would have wanted a cashmere coat, cut in classic lines to be worn over an elegant woollen dress and boots. Like Anne was wearing now.

Noticing her looking, Anne explained: 'I had to buy a few things. I couldn't keep wearing my blue skirt and fawn sweater forever. Would you like to see my new suit?'

And her three sweaters, shoes, blouses, and formal dress.

'I don't know when I'll get to wear it, but there was a sale. The shop's lease had expired. Anyway, I can wear it to the theatre and concerts. I shouldn't have spent so much because I'm saving up to travel. Adrian is helping me apply for an exchange lectureship, and Christine says I can stay with her relatives until I find my feet. They have a big house in Perugia — a villa, really.'

The quiet, withdrawn Anne had found her tongue.

Pauline held the suit against her. 'That's my colour. I've always liked pale blue.'

'Try it on', said Anne.

'You're a bit slimmer than I am. Is it size twelve?' asked Pauline, unbuttoning the coat and taking it off the hanger.

'Size ten, but a big size ten. I expect to fill out a bit now the worry is over. Put the coat on at least.'

Pauline paraded around like a mannequin, admiring herself in the mirror. 'Put the dress on, Anne. Let's see you in all your finery', she said.

Surprisingly, Anne needed no further persuasion. She took off her dress revealing a silk petticoat, and slid the black satin over her head. Gaunt suddenly became elegant. Exchanging her boots for evening slippers and clipping a single string of pearls around her neck, she stood for their admiration.

It was all too much for Eileen. She tried on the cashmere coat.

That night Eileen slept badly again. She dreamed in series, but did not really remember her dreams except for an image of Amber-Mae holding up a piece of red glass with blood dripping down her arm and splashing onto her feet. It must have been the effect of Anne's Lebanese spicy supper. She'd be fine when she'd had a shower and settled her stomach with some good Australian muesli.

'Do you realise Anne didn't have one holy picture on the wall?' said Pauline over breakfast. 'Not even a crucifix, or her favourite Catherine of Siena. Odd that. And her clothes! When Imelda left the convent she had to dress herself from opportunity shops for years. She complained about always being two years behind the fashions.'

'Remember the trafficking we used to do in holy-picture cards?' replied Eileen. 'We would give them to each other for birthdays, saints days, exams, and any other excuse we could think of. My favourite was Our Lady of the Way, because the baby looked so sweet.'

'My favourite was Our Lady of Perpetual Succour. I liked the shape of her face and the colour of her veil and dress. Another one I liked was the Divine Infant of Prague. That was one of Sister Josephine's specials. Remember how she would say: "Pray to the Divine Infant of Prague, girls, he will never let you down"?' said Pauline

'I prayed to the Divine Infant that Gerard Armstrong would break off with his girlfriend and ask me out. Every night for a whole month I stormed heaven, and Gerard was as unaware of my existence at the end of the month as he had been at the beginning. I nearly lost my faith over that one.'

'Sister Josephine would have said that it wasn't God's will for you to go out with Gerard Armstrong, desirable as he might have seemed at the time', laughed Pauline.

'Sister Josephine had all the answers.'

'I wonder how she would have felt about Anne', Pauline said as she washed up her cup and plate. 'She was her pet. Wasn't she thrilled when Anne told her she was entering?'

'She'd probably been praying to the Divine Infant of Prague about it', replied Eileen as she wiped down the table and put away the milk and margarine.

'Well, they got twenty years good service from her; that has to stand for something.'

'It was laicising our names that did it. I can't see Adrian offering his flat to Sister Mary Catherine', said Eileen.

Pauline considered for a time. 'How would you like to be still called Sister Mary Patrice?'

'No thank you! I'm not even too keen on being called Sister any more. Mind you, I did enjoy having a proper nun's name when I was first professed. Just as Clare enjoyed being Mrs Davenport when she was first married. Now she's Ms O'Grady and I'm Eileen. I wonder how Clare is getting on', she added anxiously.

'She seemed all right last time she was here. Quite over that operation thing she had. When you think about it, we all have really Catholic names: Eileen, Pauline, and Clare. And my cousin was called Carmel. No wonder you and I became nuns. We were doomed from the baptismal font.'

'You think our destinies would have been different if our parents had called us Marilyn or Diana? Sister Marilyn does not sound good, not good at all!' replied Eileen.

Pauline smiled as she hurried off in a Monday morning rush, leaving Eileen wondering. Was Pauline jealous of Anne's new lifestyle? As Sister Josephine would have said: God will not ask you if you possessed a spa bath or a cashmere coat on the Day of Judgment, but whether you were faithful to his teachings. Anne was neither closer to nor further from the kingdom of God in Adrian's flat than she had been in the suburban convent, just more comfortable.

Monday morning claimed Eileen too, and the week's whirl began. She drove to the parish church for morning mass before taking communion to patients at the local hospital. Sister Josephine would have felt upset at the thought of a woman's hands touching the sacred host. But then Sister Josephine would have had no answer to the problem of declining vocations to the priesthood, except prayer. They'd tried that. Eileen wondered if Father Tom ever had doubts about his calling. Did he feel chafed by the restrictions placed upon him by the hierarchy? Was he uneasy in his celibacy, finding the general goodwill of the whole parish no substitute for a personal, intimate relationship? She had Pauline, with whom she could share much. He had nobody except his fellow priests, whom he saw at retreats and functions. She wondered if she and Pauline should invite him around for an evening meal, but then dismissed the idea. For one thing, they only had one evening in the next fortnight where neither of them was committed to a meeting. Secondly, both she and Pauline were tired; the thought of matching Tom's cheerful energy for a whole evening made her feel even more tired. Wait until she had fully shaken off her cold and Pauline had finished all her third term corrections and reports. In the old convent they had had more time to be nuns. The world had not crowded them about. Not that she wanted to go back to being Sister Mary Patrice, whose days were strictly ordered, answering to a bell. She just needed a chance to recharge her spiritual batteries. St Teresa of Avila was always on about being in an enclosed convent, while she dashed about the countryside on her reforming missions. It was hard to be practical and recollected at the same time.

'Be ye perfect as your heavenly Father is perfect.' There was no ambiguity about that. In the meantime she had Mrs Cameron in a state of distress, Karen in a state of flux, the catechist committee in a state of conflict, the first communion and confirmation candidates in less than a prepared state to receive the sacraments, Clare needing moral support, and her mother complaining that Eileen never found time to visit her parents.

'We won't be with you forever, dear. I know you're busy, but I wouldn't like you to feel regretful if something happened to your father.'

He was starting to look a little older. There was a stoop to his shoulders and less bounce in his step than she remembered. Her mother seemed to stay the same, her silver grey hair combed and pinned back into a French roll and her hands always busy, knitting, crocheting, bottling fruit, or ministering to her beloved garden. Eileen knew, but didn't believe, that her parents would not always be there in the home she grew up in.

The usual faithful few were at the morning mass. Looking around, Eileen calculated that the average age of the daily mass attenders must have been sixty-five. What would happen when they all went to their eternal rest? She knelt in prayer after mass until the hum of conversation distracted her too much. These people all belonged to the generation that had been admonished never to talk in church. What ever had happened to their early training? She stifled her irritation. They were good, well-meaning people.

The old people at the hospital greeted her warmly. Poor old things. Most were lonely. She thought of her parents, and felt guilty. At least they had each other. Some of the old people here didn't have a visitor from one year's end to the next, except for her and a couple of parishioners. Not the same as your family.

She dropped in on Clare at lunchtime and found her busily typing more submissions for funds for the women's refuge. 'The pollies make you work for your money', Clare announced cheerfully. 'Put the kettle on and I'll join you for coffee. Are you all right? You look a bit peaky', and she went on typing without waiting for an answer.

For some inexplicable reason Eileen felt tears pricking her eyelids. She just felt tired and a bit down. Would Clare's pregnancy have been showing yet? Regrets were pointless. She wondered how it actually felt to be pregnant.

Later that afternoon she spoke to a group of mothers about the need to participate in the preparation of their children's first holy communion. 'It is important for the family to be involved. Your children's religious education is in your hands. We are just here to guide and help you.'

Mrs Merridew objected, as Eileen knew she would. 'That's why we send them to a Catholic school. The nuns taught me about the church. Isn't that what you nuns are for?'

The discussion went on and on and on. Eileen had heard it all before, countered the same objections year after year, soothed the same sense of inadequacy. Her head ached and her throat felt dry and sore. If she had a child she would love to help her prepare for first holy communion. These mothers were privileged. Thank God the school siren went and they had to collect their children and go home. Now she could do the same — minus child, of course. She decided against calling on Mrs Cameron on the way, because it was her turn to cook tea, even if she wasn't very hungry. Sister Josephine would have told her to offer up her aches and pains for the holy souls in purgatory. She wasn't sure she wouldn't rather indulge in a good bout of self-pity. Colds were horrid things.

Anne phoned that night to see if they would like to go to the pictures. Pauline had a meeting and Eileen just wanted to go to bed. She tried to concentrate on her evening prayers but it was impossible. She chose a random section of the Bible, opening up at the story of Solomon making a judgment about which mother should have custody of a baby. The true mother proved her love by being willing to give up her claim to the child. Eileen found herself thinking about Clare. She had seemed cheerful and busy, really back to her old self. It was Eileen who was suffering. Her head throbbed, nose felt stuffed up. Pauline came home and made her a hot lemon drink with honey, a remedy her mother recommended. The rare times during her novitiate when Eileen had a cold, Mother Eleanor used to bring her lemon and honey too. It slid down her throat with comforting warmth.

When Eileen called to see Mrs Cameron next day, she was pottering around the kitchen muttering to herself. A sure sign of distress. Minnie had the good sense to stay sitting on her favourite chair. Over a cup of tea, Mrs C told her the problem.

'My daughter wants me to go and live with her. She says it's a worry having me here on my own, and she wants me to make my home with her.'

'How do you feel about that?' asked Eileen.

'She's all right. Flesh and blood you can live with. But I don't really like her husband. An awful thing to say, I know, but we never did see eye to eye. He's too bossy.'

'Have they adequate room for you?' Eileen asked.

'That's just it. They haven't. She wants me to sell this house and put the money in with them so they can buy a bigger house and I can have a room to myself. I don't want to live in a room in their house. He has the television too loud. Even if I had my own television his would be too loud. And he's allergic to dogs, so he said I can't have Minnie.'

Mrs Cameron started to cry, a most uncharacteristic action, but she had been bottling up her worries for a long time. Eileen hugged her.

'You don't have to move. You don't have to sell your house. Don't cry. No-one can force you to do anything you don't want. Just tell them you don't want to go.'

'I couldn't leave my creepers. I planted them years ago, and you know how lovely the garden is in summer with the jasmine and lantana. Her garden is all bark chips and shrubs. She doesn't have a feel for plants. Like her father. The only things he could grow were vegetables, although I was grateful enough for that.'

Eileen reassured. Mrs Cameron cheered up. Released by having shared her troubles, she went into the kitchen to get more hot water for the teapot. Eileen watched her limping slightly, carrying the water with great care, and then placing the tea cosy back over the pot. Everything was in slow motion. Still, Mrs Cameron didn't have to hurry. She wasn't going anywhere.

Pentecost Sunday. Father Tom greeted the congregation at mass with a resounding 'Happy birthday', thoroughly confusing those who didn't know their church history. Pauline had invited Anne to attend the parish mass with them but she was going to an ecumenical service with Adrian and Christine. 'Who else!' remarked Eileen.

The church resembled a cross between a florist shop and an art gallery. The ladies of the parish had filled every available vase with flowers picked from their gardens or begged from friends and neighbours. Between the flower vases there were pot plants in bronze containers. Everything metal shone. The windows gleamed, the floor was polished and shiny. There was that faint smell of wax, which brought back memories.

The artistic efforts were mostly Eileen's. She had prepared cut out figures of the apostles and Mary with tongues of fire over their heads. Her Sunday school class had coloured the tongues red, and the confirmation class had finished colouring-in the figures. Amber-Mae had spent her Thursdays having a good go at a few of them, but had completed none. The figures were placed in a semicircle on the wall behind the altar.

Then there was the frieze demonstrating the seven gifts of the Holy Spirit. That dominated the front of the altar. Along the walls of the church were the names of the candidates for confirmation, each on a large sheet of paper decorated with motifs and flowers. You could tell which ones were done by the girls without even looking at the names. She had made a supreme effort, hoping to break through the feeling of lethargy and lack of interest in life. Looking around the church, she wasn't convinced it had been worth it. Did the children understand any more about the feast of Pentecost having indulged in a colouring-in extravaganza? She doubted it. Had they themselves understood when, years ago, they learnt the questions and answers from the catechism by heart? Maybe not, but she could still recite the answers.

Pauline was going to see her mother. Eileen decided to visit hers as well. They could both use the car, Pauline dropping her off and picking her up again on the way home.

Pauline wondered if her mother was happy at the home. She was clean, well-fed, and comfortable. Pauline remembered her as a bustling woman. Now she seemed more interested in looking out of the window than actually doing anything. She greeted Pauline when she visited, but showed little emotion either when she arrived or when she announced brightly that she had to leave. Poor, vacant old thing, enduring her life away. Pauline dreaded the same thing happening to her.

Eileen's parents were delighted to see her. Her mother offered her tea, cake, and remedies to 'pick her up', until her father told her to stop carrying on like an old hen. He then went outside to pick her some lemons so that she could make herself a drink if her sore throat returned. They played a three-handed game of Scrabble. Pauline arrived and stayed to watch the final scenes of a movie on television. Eileen felt reluctant to return to their community house. For two pins she would have gone to her old bedroom and refused to come out, ever. She wondered how her fellow-sister would deal with that situation!

Pauline, unaware, was having difficulty deciding if she wanted another cup of tea before they left. Eileen's mother looked tired. The lines around her eyes seemed more marked. She walked slowly towards the kitchen. Something in the way she moved made Eileen think of Mrs Cameron.

She had talked to her mother about Mrs C's dilemma. 'Poor old thing', her mother had said, not realising that she was only a few years younger than Mrs Cameron. 'Living with family seldom works out. Your Aunt Thelma moved in with some relations for a while, but then she went into a home. It's too hard. Old people don't want to live with younger ones. They have their own rhythm. Young people upset it.'

Eileen felt that her mother had put her finger on the problem. Rhythm of life. Her life was all out of kilter at the moment. Not right and fitting. Out of plumb. All those lovely metaphors. What a rich language we have, she thought, feeling slightly better. She washed up the supper dishes and stood waiting for Pauline to finish her protracted farewells and follow her to the car.

A new week, a new round of meetings and chores.

Karen had discovered an undreamt of talent for sewing. Joining a class at the Neighbourhood House, she soon had all the other students asking her to sew for them. Eileen admired a pram cover she had made for Aaron, a patchwork quilt with an abstract theme in bright colours. It made a pleasant change from teddy bears and clowns. Karen had orders to make four more. Clare had suggested that she make up a decent number and take a stall at the local Sunday market. Karen was full of this idea, throwing in the information too casually that Aaron's dad would help her with transport. Eileen hadn't realised he was coming around again on a regular basis. She hoped that Karen was being sensible.

Looking at Amber-Mae no-one would have guessed that her mother was good at sewing. Still a little ragbag. Eileen searched through the St Vincents bag for something suitable. Robbing the poor to help the poor; she was sure St Vincent wouldn't mind. Under a pile of most unpromising blue denim she found a light-blue dress with white smocking. She threw the discarded overalls and T-shirt into the laundry sink, then decided to put them in a plastic bag. She didn't mind looking after Karen's daughter, but she was blowed if she was going to do her washing as well.

Amber-Mae stood on a chair so she could see herself in the mirror. Eileen brushed her curly hair and tied it with a blue bow, using a leftover piece of ribbon from Pauline's store of bits and pieces. Did Amber-Mae realise that she was pretty? Dressed in blue and white, Our Lady's colours. Sister Josephine would have disapproved of the mirror gazing. Vanity and absorption with self. Barriers to holiness. Eileen saw it differently. Amber-Mae had been blessed with good looks, a gift from God. If her life continued in its pattern she might be burdened with many things. Let her enjoy pleasure in her own prettiness while she could.

On Tuesday morning, as she was doing a headstand, she remembered that the seminar on dealing with grief was on that morning. Thank heavens she still had a video and notes to stimulate discussion, from last year. Let's hope nobody from last year comes again, or, if they do, let's hope they have short memories, she thought.

'How do you deal with grief?' she asked Pauline over breakfast. Not the best time to discuss such a topic, but they never seemed to see each other for any length of time. Breakfast had become communication time.

'Don't know. I've never lost anybody close to me, except my father', replied Pauline, crunching her toast. Eileen had never known anyone to eat so much toast, usually plastered with Vegemite. Anne used to wrinkle her nose with disgust as she sipped at her orange juice and played with a prune, which was Anne's idea of healthy eating.

'When Dad died I just buried my feelings, I think', Pauline continued. 'I didn't accept it for a long time because I didn't see him all that often anyway. It was easy to pretend he was still there. Of course, I prayed for his soul, and when Mum visited me she talked about him a lot. I was the only person she would talk to about Dad. She always said you shouldn't burden other people with your problems. It was about a year after he died that it suddenly hit me that he was gone for good. I know I'll see him in heaven and all that, but I suddenly realised that I wouldn't see him again in this life. It was awful. Now you've started making me all morbid before the day has even started properly.' She brushed away a tear, hoping that Eileen hadn't noticed. Eileen pretended to be absorbed in pouring the tea.

Later that morning Eileen listened to other people talk about their griefs. One woman had lost a young child in horrific circumstances. She was not coping. Others had lost close friends or partners. Talking about it probably helped them. At least they were bringing their feelings out into the open. Her printed notes assured her that this was a good thing, but the video seemed inadequate in the light of these life experiences. She tried to imagine how she would feel if one of her parents, Clare, Pauline, or Amber-Mae died. How would she feel if one died violently? How would she have reacted if Clare had died because of haemorrhaging after her operation? Eileen never thought of it as anything but an 'operation'. Not even in her mind could she bring herself to say 'abortion' in connection with Clare.

The afternoon was taken up with a follow-on meeting with the first communion and confirmation parents. Their responsibilities did not cease with the reception of the sacraments. They had more worksheets and discussion groups to reinforce the good work already achieved. Eileen saw her day disappear behind a mountain of paper.

Pauline's turn to cook tea. She was in the midst of a vegetarian phase, dragging a reluctant Eileen through an array of pumpkin doodahs, unusual vegetables floating in lumpy white sauce, and burgers made from something from the health shop that promised to be a great energy source. They tasted foul. Pauline was an acceptable cook when it came to normal everyday lamb chops and steamed vegetables. Eileen wasn't all that hungry, but feared hurting the feelings of Pauline, who was munching away with every sign of enthusiasm. She even had a second helping! Eileen felt her sacrifice had been in vain. Pauline had no doubts about the success of her latest culinary creation.

The evening dragged. Eileen sat in the study preparing her final report on the catechist group. Numbers and statistics. So many confirmations. Enough first holy communions. Mother Church was alive and well in her parish. The bishop would be pleased.

Chapter Ten

Mrs Cameron had firmly told Lorraine she did not want to leave her home. Her daughter hadn't responded, but as she was leaving she said: 'I'll come around on Wednesday and take you for a drive to see a house. You might feel differently about it all then. It's in a good location. Paul thinks it would be an excellent buy.'

Mrs Cameron felt her resolve tighten. She was not going to be bullied into a 'good buy' so that Paul could wax rich and fat. Eileen, when she called later, found her in the garden inspecting the jasmine. Mrs Cameron told her about the proposed Wednesday excursion, but her chief news was about the two lovely boys from the Catholic primary school who had came around on Saturday afternoon to do some more weeding. 'They were part of the group who used to come in school time. I offered to pay them a little, but they said they didn't want any money. Isn't that something? Don't tell me that young people are all selfish. I gave them some homemade lemonade and gingerbread. Look how nice the rose bed is now!'

Eileen shared in her glow. People could be nice.

The next week the boys came back, accompanied by an older brother who offered to dig up a patch in the back garden and plant a few things. Sort of vegetables he called them. Mrs Cameron offered to water them for him each day, an offer which he gratefully accepted.

The plants flourished. The two younger boys, Graeme and Peter, came every now and again. They loved mowing the lawn with the old hand mower and watering the garden, chasing each other about. Mrs Cameron turned a blind eye to their capers with the hose, reflecting that boys would be boys. The sound of their laughter made her think of her brothers, when they were all young, back in Scotland. She made shortbread for the boys.

Lorraine continued to take her for drives to look at houses, always returning to the one Paul favoured. Mrs Cameron had to admit that it had a big garden, and was near the shops although in a quiet street. A great house for Paul, Lorraine and family. She just didn't want any part of it. 'The children would love to have all that space', said Lorraine, trying to make her feel guilty. Mrs Cameron said she felt sure that they would, as she gazed placidly out of the car window, untroubled by any stronger feeling than the desire for a cup of tea.

Clare started to look louder. Her hair became a shade of 'wild scarlet', as her mother called it. Earrings dangled and clanged; multi-coloured jumpsuit. Even her voice boomed. Eileen wasn't sure she liked the new Clare.

Only once did she refer to the abortion. 'It would have been born soon. Wonder if it was a boy or girl.'

'It's a little saint in heaven now', replied Eileen.

'You really believe all that antiquated rubbish', commented Clare. 'If it is in heaven with God, as you say, it will be thanking me for saving it a lot of misery first. Anyway, it wasn't baptised.'

Then she turned her attention to the reason she had called. She wanted Eileen to run a meditation course at the refuge. 'Those women need to learn to relax. Poor bitches. They live their lives on the edge.'

Was it orthodox feminism to call women 'bitches'?

'Meditation's something you work up to. You have to be in the right frame of mind. Are they Catholics?' said Eileen.

Clare stared at her. 'What on earth has that got to do with it? Do you think Catholics are the only ones who meditate? Don't you do yoga?'

'Yes, every morning.'

'But you aren't Hindu', said Clare triumphantly.

Eileen wanted to explain that meditation is something you come to, not something you do. At least she thought she might be able to help the women to cope a little with their chaotic emotions. She imagined that anyone driven to seek shelter in the overcrowded confines of Clare's women's refuge must be pretty desperate. There might be sanctuary there, but seldom serenity.

Next time she called, Mrs Cameron had a story to tell her. The police had been! They had wanted to question her about some plants in her backyard. 'The wicked rascals', she chuckled. 'I thought they were odd-looking vegetables.'

Eileen was shocked. She thought Mrs C must be devastated and disillusioned. She might have been arrested!

Mrs Cameron didn't see it quite that way. She was highly amused. 'Just like my brother, he was. Always up to some scheme or other. I'd like to know what the police did with the plants, too. They packed them away very carefully, and I heard one saying they had good heads on them.'

Eileen was shocked again. Mrs Cameron seemed such a nice old lady.

'I suppose the young boys won't be back now. I'll miss them. See how lovely the rose-garden is where they weeded it. I gave them a bunch of roses for their mother.'

Mrs Cameron chattered on. Eileen had a sudden sense of being back in the old convent garden with Sister Celine, admiring her roses as she picked them for Our Lady's altar. She felt a yearning to be back there, peaceful and secure. The longing was a pain in her soul. She imagined the faint cypressy scent of the trees along the driveway, the cool corner of the grotto, ferns growing at Bernadette's feet. It was the almost forgotten feeling of homesickness.

Karen arrived as usual with Amber-Mae on Thursday morning. She no longer attended classes, but, while Eileen made no objection, she saw no reason to change the arrangement. It gave her a few hours respite from the child, a chance to do some sewing and a bit of housework. She was going through a tidy phase that would probably last as long as the not smoking, which had petered out after a month. Still, she was smoking less now than she used to, as she assured a disappointed Eileen, who was horrified at the thought of the two children being subjected to passive smoking. What Eileen did to her lungs was her own concern.

Amber-Mae ran to greet her, a smile lighting up her face and her hand outstretched to clasp Eileen's. They went straight into the spare room, which both Pauline and Eileen called 'my study'.

Amber-Mae knew the routine. She settled herself on a chair after Eileen had put a cushion on it so that she could reach the table. White paper and crayons awaited her, and she was happy. Eileen made admiring responses from time to time as the child held up her squiggles for inspection. Today she was making a birthday card for Karen. Last week it had been a 'pretty picture for Mummy'. Karen was usually too busy talking to Eileen or rearranging Aaron in his pram to take much notice of the proffered gift. Maybe she puts them on a display board at home, thought Eileen without conviction. She didn't often visit there now, as she saw Karen once a week at the convent. She didn't realise, until Karen told her, that Aaron's father, Jimmy, had moved back in.

'I've got an IUD now, so it's all right', Karen assured her, as though that were the only point to consider. 'I'm not going to be that stupid again.'

Now that she had broken the news, the floodgates opened. Grammar was sacrificed. Did truth fare better? 'He's part Abo, you know. Doesn't really look it if you didn't know already. Know what I mean? He and Amber-Mae's dad had a big fight, years ago. We was at the pub, and Eddy — that's Amber-Mae's dad — reckoned he was looking at me. Anyways, they had a big fight outside the pub. Eddy started it, but the cops came and stuck Jimmy in the cells. He got time for that. Bloody Eddy wasn't even arrested. Trust the pigs. I felt sorry for Jimmy. It was sort of my fault.'

Plump, cheerful, seventeen-year-old Karen, already a mother, having two men fight over her at the pub. Had there been romance in her life after all?

'That bastard Eddy shot through a month later. Reckoned I was a slut. He could talk!'

Karen stopped to check if Eileen was shocked. Eileen nodded companionably, so she continued. 'When Jimmy come out of jail, he come round to see us. Reckoned he was going to bash Eddy's head in, only Eddy wasn't there. That's how Aaron got here.'

There had to be a connection between an aggressive Jimmy on the doorstep and the conception of Aaron. Although Eileen couldn't quite see it, she felt that asking for further details would add confusion rather than lucidity to the story. What did it matter? Aaron was here, and Jimmy now wanted to be a 'proper father'.

'He drinks a bit, but he's all right. He's painting Aaron's bedroom and I'm making new curtains, like the cot cover. It should look beaut when it's finished.'

Eileen had to ask. 'How does he get on with Amber-Mae?'

'Not too good, Sister. He doesn't hit her or nothing, but, see, she's Eddy's kid and he hates Eddy. And she seems to go out of her way to bug him. I get that mad at her sometimes I have to send her out of the room. She can be a real pain when she wants.'

Poor little Amber-Mae. What hope did she have against the combined attractions of Jimmy, Aaron, and painted bedrooms? Wild ideas went through Eileen's head. Let Amber-Mae come and stay with her. She could have the spare room. In the old days convents often had orphans foisted upon them. Look at Anne. Pauline wouldn't mind, she thought. Then, even Eileen in her desperation had to admit that this was not true.

Maybe her mother and father could adopt her? A child around the house would rejuvenate them. Or what about Clare? There must be someone who would love and care for Amber-Mae. She'd have to pray about it. Top of the list.

It should have been easy to tell Clare that she didn't want to come to the refuge and take a session on meditation. All she had to say was no. Sounds simple; with Clare, almost impossible. She didn't hear that particular word very well, and Eileen was still learning how to say it. So she set off on the designated morning, a sense of impending failure making her journey through the traffic more troublesome than usual. To calm her feelings she played Hildegarde of Bingen's music. She would have coped with modern living. Probably have become head of the United Nations. Hildegarde would have known how to say no, not allowing herself to be browbeaten into an unpalatable task that undoubtedly would turn out to be a complete fiasco. Eileen knew that God loves us all equally, but some people are more attuned to meditation than others, and the rough, tough women of Clare's shelter did not sound likely candidates.

Had Eileen thought the matter through, she would have realised that the women who found their way to the refuge were victims. Far from being rough and tough, they were defeated and frightened. Clare needed her determination to support them in further action, as making the dash to the refuge had taken all their courage and resourcefulness. Some inkling of this came to Eileen as she looked around the small group. Five women and a child who clung to her mother and refused to join the other children in the playroom. Five women, one with severe bruising on her face, one defiantly chewing gum, and the others looking passively at Eileen, waiting to see what she had to deliver. Dear God, she thought, how do I get through to them?

Hildegarde helped. Placing the tape, which she always carried in her handbag, in the cassette player, she let the gentle music work its magic on them. The little girl stopped whining, struggled onto her mother's lap, and, with her head against the maternal skinny bosom, went to sleep.

Eileen told them about Hildegarde, who had run an abbey famed throughout Europe, advised popes and princes, and been a scholar and visionary. She hoped they felt inspired.

Stop dodging the issue, she thought to herself. You are here to teach them meditation, not waffle on about holy women who lived centuries ago. So they began. Eileen talked a little about the need to find the stillness within oneself.

'Sit in a comfortable position', she said. 'Close your eyes. Don't try to think about anything in particular. Just choose a word or phrase. One which has meaning for you. It may be 'peace', or 'love', or 'God our Parent'. Repeat this to yourself, over and over.'

'Like a mantra?' asked the woman with the bruised face.

Eileen, surprised, agreed that that was exactly what it was.

They sat, eyes closed, presumably repeating their mantra to themselves. Eileen didn't dare close her eyes in case they pulled faces at her, or yawned and walked out. She had visions of opening her eyes to an empty room.

Afterwards, over coffee, Clare said she was delighted with the results. She could see people were calmer already, and even little Bianca had stayed asleep when her mother carried her off to her bed.

'That child hasn't slept properly since she came here', Clare told her. 'She was so tense and miserable. Now look at her. This could be the turning point.'

Dear Clare, always enthusiastic and optimistic. Eileen thought that the women had gained a little in knowledge and had had a quiet half-hour, but she didn't really think she had changed their lives.

Pauline, hearing about it later, said she had tried similar sessions with the year 11 and 12 girls. 'They all like the idea of meditation. That's trendy. Sitting still isn't. I use tapes and slides, but that rather defeats the purpose. They have to be doing things all the time.'

Just being, joined with a rhythm to our lives. Was that the solution, Eileen wondered. Sounded like a prescription for a contemplative order. She should have been a Carmelite!

Pauline thought that being a Carmelite would be incredibly tedious. 'Imagine getting up at exactly the same time every day of your life, saying the same prayers, sitting next to the same people, year in year out. It doesn't bear thinking about.' She shuddered.

'What about peace and security in the certainty that you allowed nothing to come between you and God? You read the life of Teresa of Avila. She was half in heaven for most of her life', replied Eileen.

'Lot of good it did her', grumped Pauline, who had no time for histrionics. You showed what you were by what you did. Retiring to her room to play the flute, she thought no more about it.

Eileen loved to read about the lives of the contemplative saints. No delicate submission about them. They seemed to win favours from God by stubbornness and great love. All of their lives contained suffering through sickness, being misunderstood, or taking on a life of penance and self-denial. That led her to the thought that the bishop really didn't understand her. But he didn't seem to understand many people.

Eileen sighed. She was not obsessed with love for God. Not like Teresa of Avila or Clare of Assisi. She allowed herself to be distracted by unimportant things like chilblains.

Obsession. Was that the key?

Pauline's flute played gently in the background. Not the instrument she would have chosen for Pauline. That thought set her matching people with instruments. Clare should play the oboe, Karen the bassoon. Her mother would suit a cello, her father a French horn. Her brother, whom she hadn't seen for years, needed a piano on which to play vigorously. Herself she fancied at the harp, gently plucking the strings as cascades of beautiful sound filled the room. Had she chosen a harp, subconsciously, for its celestial connotations? She smiled faintly at the thought, while feeling slightly irritated. She couldn't even have a fun mental game without the whole thing becoming subjective. She wasn't obsessed with love for God. She was obsessed with love for herself. That realisation made her think suddenly of Sister Josephine. Would she have understood the concept of learning to love ourselves before we can learn to love others? Not even Mother Eleanor, for all her sweet practical wisdom, would have approved of that idea.

Clare insisted that the meditation sessions continue. Eileen complained that she didn't really have time, but she found time all the same. Some weeks were more successful than others. It was a constantly changing clientele, so she couldn't build from week to week. The coffee session afterwards was always an eye-opener. Eileen had been a parish worker for a number of years, helping people in distress and through bad patches, but she had never encountered the misery and hopelessness that some of these women described. The anguish at seeing teenage children refuse to go to mass didn't rate against the horror of knowing that your husband had been forcing your daughter to have sex with him for years. In your family home, sometimes while you were in the kitchen preparing a meal. Some of Eileen's parishioners knew poverty, but none that she knew had resorted to prostitution to pay for the children's food. If they did, they didn't tell her about it.

Not all of Clare's women were refugees from horror. Some had just become fed up with marriage, with the submissive role into which society and their husbands had cast them. They read one inflammatory feminist article too many, and fled to the refuge to be bolstered and thumped between the shoulder blades by a supportive Clare.

'I knew my marriage was a mistake on the honeymoon', explained one. 'I wanted to leave then, but I thought, "What will my mother say?" It took me six years to make the break.'

'What was wrong with him?' another women asked. Husbands or

lovers were always 'him'. Men didn't have names in the refuge.

'He wanted to dominate me. He wanted to control everything I did. He used to sit and stare at me while I ate!'

Eileen felt, again, that she hadn't missed all that much by not being married. The more she listened to these women the more reconciled she became to the whole idea of celibacy. Not that she regretted her vocation, but in choosing one way of life she had of necessity turned her back on another, and she had to admit to a certain curiosity about what she had never experienced. Motherhood was another matter. She could never pretend to herself that she had not yearned for that experience. So much longing for the impossible.

Our Lady, Virgin and Mother. The best of both worlds. Was that a disrespectful thought? Mary would understand that she didn't mean to be rude; she was just tired and disgruntled.

Clare started having lots of men-friends, discarded one after the other. 'Too wimpy', 'idealogically unsound', or, to shock Eileen, 'he snored'.

Anne sent a postcard from Greece and promised to write a longer letter from Rome. Eileen wished she had the chance to see all those places. Rome, Florence, Venice, Naples. She knew of two nuns who had been allowed a year off to travel through Europe with their widowed mother. They never returned to the convent.

'Five hundred dollars. That's all it would take. We'd pay you back.' Karen and Jimmy wanted to buy tools and materials to make wooden cradles and sell them at the market.

Eileen explained to Karen that, while she thought the idea a good one, she just didn't have any money. Not that sort of money. Karen looked unconvinced. Jimmy had told her that the Catholic church had more money than it knew what to do with. 'Look at all their buildings; they own all that property right in the middle of the city. And the pope is always travelling round the place. Takes money for that. They should have a bit to help us out. We're battlers.' So he had explained. So she had asked. Eileen felt sorry for them. But the church's riches had not filtered down to her. They would have to apply elsewhere.

'Where?' asked Karen.

'Try the bank, or doesn't the government have schemes for things like that? I could try and find out', answered Eileen somewhat lamely.

Karen said 'Hmmph', and later borrowed the money from Clare, who had organised a self-help fund at the refuge. She seemed to bear Eileen no ill will, reporting in a short time that their stall at the market was going 'real well' and they were 'that busy she didn't know if she was Arthur or Martha'.

Chapter Eleven

The phone shrilling through the quiet, dark house brought both Eileen and Pauline running. Even in the confusion Eileen noticed with some amusement that Pauline had her hair in curlers.

An unfamiliar female voice apologised for calling Eileen so late. An emergency.

The story took its telling all the same.

'I live next door to Mrs Cameron. The poor dear. Used to worry about her something shocking, living on her own like that. Told her to bang on the wall if she ever needed help. Last week she did bang on the wall, so I went rushing in. Right in the middle of cooking dinner, but she was only hammering in a picture hook. So the next time I didn't take that much notice, only Minnie started howling. I went in and there she was, Mrs Cameron, lying on the kitchen floor. She'd slipped on something and fallen. Broke her ribs, the ambulance man said, most probably. She asked me to call you. Not her daughter. She wanted you, and can you take Minnie as well. I can't. Minnie fights with our poodle.'

Eileen sifted the relevant details. Early next morning she went to the hospital to find Mrs Cameron huddled in the large hospital bed. Eileen sat down beside her. The old lady clung to her hand. They stayed like that while Eileen prayed for healing. She noted Mrs Cameron's face showed a little colour. She seemed more serene.

Firm high-heeled steps sounded down the corridor.

'I knew something like this would happen! How are you, mother?' Lorraine didn't exactly tell Eileen to go home, just pretended that she wasn't there. Leaning over her to place flowers in a vase, she settled on the chair opposite to where Eileen was sitting and proceeded to talk. Mrs Cameron shrank further into the blankets. Eileen stood, or rather, sat her ground. She would not abandon Mrs C in her time of need.

The arrival of the doctor broke the impasse. Eileen said she had to go. Lorraine said she had to talk to the doctor after he had examined her mother. There were things to discuss.

She's like a crow, a sleek, gloating crow, thought Eileen, not even bothering to worry about being uncharitable. She was too upset for Mrs Cameron, who had spent hours lying in pain, unable to reach the phone, just managing, eventually, to drag herself to a wall where she could summon help. Not that help was swift. If Minnie hadn't started howling, how much longer would she have lain there? Poor lady, what a shocking experience.

Eileen had lots to do, but she took time to visit her own mother and talk about it all. She needed the sympathetic audience, the shared cup of tea, to reassure herself that her parents were all right. Bookwork could wait.

Pauline was sympathetic too when she heard the rest of the story. Minnie was welcomed, 'for a little while, and not in the house'.

Minnie fretted. A forlorn figure on the back mat, staring glumly at her plate of dried food. Eileen tried tinned meat, then delicacies from the butcher. Minnie picked delicately at minced steak while Pauline threatened her with stories of the starving millions, until the dog silenced her with sad eyes.

Eileen did the unthinkable. She smuggled a squirming Minnie into hospital. Mrs Cameron gave a cry of delight when she saw Minnie's face peering over the top of a large basket. The dog leapt out straight onto the bed into Mrs Cameron's waiting arms.

Omnipotent matron saw, condemned. Minnie was never to return; Eileen, maybe. Mrs Cameron cried and cried. Eileen, deeply upset, allowed Minnie to sleep on her bed at home, ignoring Pauline's protests.

A few days later Mrs C was feeling chirpier. 'The doctors said there's not much you can do with broken ribs except rest them. They are keeping me in for a few more days.' She leaned forward, a conspirator. 'Lorraine can't make me go home to her place if I have domiciliary care and Meals on Wheels. And you drop in regularly, don't you.' It was a statement, not a question.

Mrs Cameron had always scorned Meals on Wheels. That was for people who were too lazy to grow a few vegetables and cook for themselves. It was a measure of her desperation that she looked on the scheme as her salvation.

Lorraine didn't give in easily. She enlisted nurses and social workers in her cause. Doctors, peering gravely over spectacles, assured Mrs C that she would be better off with constant supervision. Just in case.

'Makes me sound like a simpleton', Mrs Cameron objected. 'Constant supervision! Who wants to be supervised? I can stay at home. That's supervision enough. Lorraine used to be too busy to bother with me. Now she's not busy enough. Needs something to occupy her.'

Eileen and the hospital social worker helped make the arrangements. Mrs Cameron was ready to go home.

Her daughter, accepting defeat, offered to drive her when she was discharged from hospital. Eileen felt it more tactful to stay away, promising to deliver a freshly bathed Minnie, tartan ribbon around her neck, when Mrs Cameron was settled.

This time it was Lorraine who telephoned. Pauline took the message. 'It seems your Mrs Cameron slipped as she was going down the hospital steps. Broke her hip, the daughter said. Wanted to know if we could keep Minnie for a bit longer. Says she'll take her to the Animal Welfare as soon as she can manage it. I told her we didn't mind having Minnie for a few more days.'

Eileen untied the ribbon, absentmindedly patting Minnie.

Forget about Animal Welfare, Lorraine, she thought. Are you planning to take your mother there at the same time? Solve all your problems in one fell swoop?

Clare gave up men-friends after she met Lilian, described by Clare as being 'straight from the pages of D.H. Lawrence', a description which disturbed Pauline more than a little. 'You don't think they are . . .?' She dared the question, but not in its entirety.

Eileen snapped back: 'How should I know, and it's none of our business anyway'.

Clare talked about it quite frankly. She had never felt closer to anyone than Lilian, who had given her life a new dimension. If Eileen couldn't accept their relationship she didn't want her as a sister.

Eileen felt incredibly hurt.

Surprisingly, she was quite comfortable with Lilian. A woman who managed to achieve what she wanted by convincing others that that was how it should be. Without bully or bombast. A leader among persons. She and Clare helped a group of residents from the high-rise flats set up a shopping cooperative. Eileen suggested St Vincents do the same for the parish, but Father Tom, while approving the concept, worried about offending the local business that supported them so well. Eileen suggested a food bank then, collecting products that would otherwide have been thrown away, and distributing them to the needy. Father Tom thought that was beyond their scope.

'It's no good suggesting things', said Pauline. 'You have to do it yourself.'

'It's a matter of time. I can't do everything myself', replied Eileen, who was terrified at the idea of approaching shopkeepers and organising transport. She needed a Lilian to inspire her.

'I know what you mean', agreed Pauline. 'I'd help you if I had time, but there just aren't enough hours in a day.'

'Give us this day our daily bread', they prayed that evening.

'And give others their daily bread too', prayed Eileen. 'And forgive me for not doing more about it. For not going out into the streets at night with warm soup and sandwiches for the homeless people who sleep under bridges. Forgive me for living in a land of plenty and not moving heaven and earth to share my wealth with those who hunger and thirst. Forgive me, Lord, for seeking your kingdom in the safety of familiar places.'

She went to bed thinking of Mrs Cameron, whose leg was not healing as quickly as the doctor had hoped. Lorraine showed concern. She also offered to supervise the sale of her mother's house while she was in hospital, to save her all the anxiety. Mrs Cameron said, 'We'll see', but Eileen could see she was weakening. Looked at objectively, what choice did she have?

Pauline thought she was lucky to have a daughter prepared to look after her. 'I'd hate to see her in a home like the one my mother is in. They look after you, but it kills the spirit.'

Eileen wasn't totally surprised when Mrs C asked her about the spare room. 'I could still have domiciliary care and Meals on Wheels. It's just that I'd have someone there for a bit, until I'm ready to go back home. It would only be for a little while.'

Tears of humiliation shone in her eyes. Eileen understood what it cost to ask, and promised to discuss it with Pauline. 'I can't make a decision like that off my own bat', she explained. 'We are a community, and what affects us both has to be agreed together.'

Pauline was sympathetic but adamant. They were there to serve God's people, not be nursemaids to one old lady who had, when all was said and done, a daughter willing to look after her. And while they were on the subject, how long was Minnie staying with them?

Mrs Cameron understood. It had been her only hope or she wouldn't have asked.

Within a month she was dead.

Chapter Twelve

Eileen became more and more irritated by Pauline. Just little things, nothing you could really complain about. Pauline left her used teabag on the sink, played the same tune over and over on her flute. She thought about St Thérèse, the Little Flower, who used to seek out irritating members of the community at recreation as part of her quest for sanctity. Frankly, Eileen couldn't see that offering Pauline up was going to solve the problem.

Maybe they had been together too long, or maybe they needed Anne as a buffer. Probably Pauline found living with her irksome as well.

She was still upset over Mrs Cameron's death, even though she had been an old lady who had died peacefully. Gone to sleep one night and not woken up in the morning. Eileen had brought her communion two days before. According to the scheme of things she had now found eternal rest.

Minnie stayed with them. As though sensing her mistress's death, she lost what little bounce she had previously shown, sleeping the day away on the front verandah.

'She might as well stay. She'll be protection', said Pauline.

They had both laughed at the absurdity of the idea, and for a while the tension relaxed.

Eileen knew that Pauline had her own problems. She was, after all, in charge of religion in a large secondary college. 'The way I see it, we have to teach the girls to be open to God's love and guidance. Evangelisation, not indoctrination. All they want is to talk about their relationship problems. Mostly problems with boys. I feel like telling them to forget it for a few years, but I know I'd lose them completely if I said that.'

Eileen sympathised. 'The world is changing all the time', she said. 'We have to judge how far we should change with it. Today young people probably know more about sex than we ever will, although I must admit the television is becoming a great teacher.'

'But no-one seems to enjoy lovemaking. Watch it on television and it seems to be jolly hard work and not much fun', replied Pauline

'Clare says it's overrated', answered Eileen as she left the room.

Eileen didn't want to talk about sex any more. She felt embarrassed. Pauline had no such inhibitions. She even laughed at jokes which Eileen had trouble understanding. That's what came from mixing with adolescent girls who knew the lot.

She, on the other hand, tried for an objective knowledge. No good pretending she wasn't a sexual being. That was the way God had made her, intending her to be a complete, fulfilled woman. But she didn't need to dwell on the subject. A person on a diet doesn't spend hours looking at a cookbook.

Her sexuality, whatever that was, was channelled into her vocation. Had she been asked to explain what that meant, she couldn't have.

She no longer thought of her virginity as a precious object which she delivered, carefully wrapped, to St Peter at the gates of heaven when she died. Neither had she had any desire to explore the so called 'third way' so popular with the clergy after Vatican II. Being part of the universe, part of God's plan for the world — that made her feel creative. Her focus was towards Good, not a particular person. Sex she knew about, love she experienced. Those who claimed she had missed out on one of life's great experiences might be right. She would never know.

Clare and Lilian came around the afternoon after Mrs Cameron's funeral to show off their new touring bikes. Pauline insisted on a trial run down the road and through the bike tracks in the park. Lilian went with her. Clare and Eileen sat on the edge of the gutter, waiting for them to return.

'Have you seen Karen lately?' Clare asked.

'Not for a few weeks. How is the market stall going?'

'That's fine. But I'm worried about her — and Amber-Mae. My social-worker friend told me that they are investigating complaints that Amber-Mae is being physically abused. A creche worker reported finding bruises on her arms and back. She's got her nervous squint back too. Why she let that creep Jimmy back in I'll never know.'

Eileen drove around to Karen's house the next day as soon as she had finished the meeting that had followed the parish morning mass, visited the woman who was responsible for organising the catechists roster, ordered the film for a seminar on the sacraments, and had a rushed lunch. Karen was just going out as she got there, Aaron tucked in his pram, and Amber-Mae holding the handle. The little girl smiled a shy welcome. Karen didn't.

'Long time no see', Karen said. 'Come to stick your nose in like everybody else? Well, we're fine. Come on, Amber-Mae.'

With surprising speed she pushed the pram up the hill, away from Eileen. Amber-Mae struggled to keep up while turning a puzzled face around to look at Eileen.

She talked it over with Pauline that evening as they ate their evening meal, this being one of the few nights neither had a meeting. Pauline was a comfort. 'Now that Karen has developed self-confidence, she feels able to be rude and aggressive towards the people who helped her. I see it all the time at school.'

In the gospel according to Pauline everything happened at school.

'I couldn't see any bruises on Amber-Mae, but I didn't have much of a chance. She was whisked away so quickly.'

'Exactly. There's method in Karen's rudeness. Didn't Clare say the social workers are on to it? You don't really have to do anything.'

But Eileen wanted to do something. She felt extreme distress to think of Amber-Mae being knocked about. She missed the little girl's visits, even if she did occasionally draw on the walls. It was about time Clare had some grandchildren.

This final thought was dismissed as being totally irrational. Clare's children were far too young to marry, and if they did produce children there was no guarantee that they would be any more appealing than themselves. It was the first time she admitted to herself that she didn't like Clare's children. She suspected that neither did Clare.

Pauline spoke again. 'Let's have a day off next week to do something just for ourselves. It's a professional development day next Wednesday, which is really a catch-up day for the teachers. I'll make sure I'm caught up and you can clear the day of duties. We both need a bit of fun in our lives.'

Whatever had she been reading lately? Matthew Fox, probably.

Wednesday would be a day of ecstasies, when they would whee whee their way all the way to the beach or cinema, stroll through the Botanical Gardens, and have a meal at the local Pizza Palace. Pizza was their height of decadence.

They had an absorbing evening planning. It would have taken a week to do all the things they considered as possibilities. Not to worry. Half the fun was in the planning.

Later, as they said their community evening prayers, Eileen thanked God for Pauline's friendship, but silently. She didn't want to embarrass her.

Next morning she rang Clare to ask about Karen and Amber-Mae, not wishing another rebuff. Clare knew little. She was waiting on a copy of the report from her social-worker friend, who, she said, was very overworked and always behind on her paperwork.

'Perhaps she is hoping the people will have found a solution by the time she finishes writing about it, and then nothing will have to be done', suggested Eileen.

The remark was not appreciated.

Clare did know that her friend had visited and had found Karen rather belligerent and Jimmy very drunk. Amber-Mae had had a bruise on her leg, but you couldn't put a child into foster care for one bruise.

Foster care!

Eileen decided to visit Karen first thing in the morning, whatever the reception might be.

Karen greeted her cheerfully, as though the other day had never happened. The house was clean and tidy. Amber-Mae clung to her mother instead of running over to Eileen as she used to do.

'We are thinking of going to the country. Jimmy's family is up there. He reckons they're good people. We're sick of busybodies sticking their noses into our business when they're not wanted. Oh, I don't mean you, Sister. You're OK.'

'What about your stall?' Eileen asked somewhat desperately.

'We can still come down once a month for that, and a couple of shops have given us orders. It doesn't bring in a lot but it's a help. Drinking money. We still need the dole. Stop that, Amber-Mae!' she concluded, giving the little girl a sharp shake. 'We might go real soon.'

'I hope you won't go without saying goodbye', said Eileen.

'Of course not. You can come to our farewell party.' Karen suddenly realised what she had said. 'Perhaps you'd better not. It might get a bit rough. Jimmy's friends like to drink.'

Amber-Mae sidled up to Eileen holding out a piece of paper on which she had drawn a few lines in red crayon. 'For you', she said. 'It's a present for you.'

Eileen went to lift the child onto her knee, but Karen snatched her back and told her to look after Aaron, who was crawling about the kitchen clanging saucepan lids together.

Eileen left the house feeling no happier than when she had arrived.

Chapter Thirteen

Anne wrote to them quite regularly, newsy letters full of her exhilaration with a new lifestyle, travel, and study. Pauline and Eileen wondered if she would get married.

'Not at her age', said Eileen.

'Not the type', said Pauline, who was a romantic. She once told Eileen she had been a little bit in love many times, but never deeply enough to allow it to disturb her.

Eileen had never been really in love, although she admitted to herself that she had become rather fond of the father of one of her students. The girl had left school and she never saw the man again, but she remembered the lurch in her stomach whenever she saw him, and the disappointment when his wife turned up for a parent-teacher interview. Love's a perfectly natural thing, she told herself, and one to which many people attach a great deal of importance.

When Jesus urged us to seek the kingdom of God did he mean us to go to so many meetings? Eileen wondered as she drove towards the civic centre for the annual general meeting of the Relief Housing Scheme as the parish representative on the board of management. This was to be no ordinary meeting. Allegations had been made that the coordinator had pocketed some of the rent money instead of banking it as all good coordinators should. Proof was offered in the form of a new car which she had acquired some months ago. Further proof was the fact that only three hundred dollars rent money had been banked, when anybody could calculate that three emergency houses rented out at forty dollars a week came to much more than three hundred dollars a year.

The coordinator, Irene, now ex-coordinator, claimed that most of the tenants hadn't paid their rent. They were people in crisis, struggling to pay for their food and essential items. Rent was low on the list of priorities.

Eileen wished she wasn't involved. Too much nastiness.

The board had polarised into two factions. Richard and Jacinta for Irene, whom they saw as a caring and dedicated worker, sat at one end of the table. Fronting them were Mandy, Fiona, and Sarah, strong supporters of looking facts in the face, knowing something shifty had been going on for a long time, and cooperating with the authorities. Eileen sat somewhere in the middle.

The authorities had been busy. Police had collected a pile of badly kept account books and testimonies from cowed tenants —

who assured anyone who would listen that they had paid their rent, not only on the dot but ahead of time — and had delivered them to the Crown Prosecutor's Office.

Something had gone badly awry. A scheme to temporarily house homeless people, help them to find permanent accommodation, and put their lives into order shouldn't have ended in acrimony, accusations, and withdrawal of funding for the scheme. Eileen had liked Irene, got on well with her, and found it hard to believe that she had been dishonest.

The new coordinator, Doreen, tried to stay neutral. There but for the grace, and all that sort of thing. Eileen wondered if she had been chosen simply because she was the direct opposite of Irene. Where one was forthright and never afraid to express her point of view, the other was quiet, seldom disagreeing with the stronger members of the committee. But then, nobody else disagreed with them much either. Doreen looked like a small possum perched at the end of the table, with her report and account books neatly stacked in front of her.

Eileen wished she wasn't there.

'Might I make a suggestion?' she said. 'Let us confine the conversation to present matters and leave the unfortunate affair of Irene to be settled in the courts. I believe her case is coming up next month.'

Everyone agreed that this was a sensible suggestion. They continued to talk about Irene at considerable length. The chairperson, having vented her spleen, finally glanced at her watch, called the meeting to order, and officially opened proceedings.

Possum Doreen had managed to collect an impressive amount of rent, although the people in 14 Stratford St were proving difficult. She was working on it, although they did have six children supported by a single unemployed parent. Irene would have been round there teaching them how to make nourishing soup, and going shopping with them in the market, haranguing the stall keepers to give them extra fruit and vegetables. Nor did she allow her vegetarian principles to stop her working on the butcher for any spare meat he couldn't sell. Eileen smiled to think of Irene in a court of law, probably telling the judge how to improve courtroom procedures and offering advice to various members of the jury.

Returning from the meeting she felt tired, cross, and her back hurt. There weren't enough hours in the day to fit in all she had to do, yet what she did seemed so trivial sometimes. Her life was made up of a succession of jabs at things, but nothing ever seemed to get done. Not to a satisfactory conclusion. The meeting had ended without any specific results. Those who had thought that Irene was innocent still believed in her. Those who believed that nobody would be so incompetent at bookkeeping, unless she wanted to create a muddle as a smokescreen, smiled with cynical indulgence. Eileen wondered how much time they had left to care for the homeless people who looked to their organisation to find them emergency shelter. These winter nights were chill. As she snuggled under her blanket she felt guilty thinking of those who were sleeping in the streets. Did they not feel the cold as much? Surely they were inured to it. The alcoholics slept in a state of miserable inebriation, oblivious to the elements, or so she believed. Were they sober enough in the morning to register the frost?

Pauline's attitude to the whole affair was that it was best not to be involved. Once you allowed yourself to become emotional your judgment was clouded.

Christ wept over Jerusalem. Was that with complete detachment? Eileen asked. She decided to go and visit Irene, but never quite seemed to find the time to drive over to the other side of town.

It was time for Father Tom's annual holiday. The parish bulletin contained the information that Sister Eileen would be in charge of the parish while he was away. This meant handing on emergency phone messages to priests from neighbouring parishes, overseeing the administration of the parish (which could run itself quite successfully, as far as she could see) and announcing the urgent messages at the end of each mass. Lamington drives, catechists meetings, school camps. Things like that. Eileen hated the sound of her voice over the microphone. Now that they were wired for sound there was no need for the big-voiced priests who used to roar and harangue their parishioners cowering in the wooden pews. No wonder the message had softened. Hell and guilt were out. Opening yourself to God's guidance and community spirit were in. The only thing that hadn't changed were the lamingtons. During those two weeks she enjoyed the feeling that she was in charge.

The day of Irene's court case drew nearer. The board of management buzzed with renewed zest.

Richard was approached by Irene's solicitor. He knew about the hardship cases, the ones who couldn't pay rent. He had told Irene he would do all he could to establish her innocence.

Except appear in court, it seemed. Law courts made him very nervous. Seeing Eileen after Sunday mass he explained his dilemma, hoping for her sympathy. 'I don't want to be involved. It's as simple as that. You can call me a moral coward if you like, but the thought of giving evidence in court terrifies me. My wife understands how I feel', he finished lamely, as Eileen's expression indicated that she did not.

'What about truth and justice?' she asked, 'or don't you want to get involved with them either?'

She turned away to hide the tears of anger in her eyes. Why did Tom have to pick this time to be away? He would talk some sense into this wimp.

Where were you when I needed your evidence? she muttered. Hiding behind your wife's understanding, that's where. It warmed my heart as I sat in my prison cell to think of such a united couple. Her anger grew. Christian charity struggled for a toehold, and lost.

'Look at this!' exclaimed Pauline next evening, waving about a newspaper. When she held it still long enough for Eileen to focus she saw the headline: **Ms Robin Hood charged with theft**, under which a blurred photograph of Irene featured.

'Let me read it', she said, almost snatching the paper from Pauline.

The journalists had adopted Irene as their holy cause for the week. Heart-rending tales of tenants who had been saved from certain death in the chilly winter nights. Families who had despaired of ever 'making a go of it' bared their indignation to reporters who elaborated on the disgraceful treatment of their benefactress.

The saga continued next day. One letter to the editor stated that it was symptomatic of our country's ills that a woman was praised in the daily paper for allowing the unemployed to milk the system even further. This letter was flanked by others lauding the humanity, kindness, and charity of Irene, now a victim of bureaucracy.

'You would think she had opened up her own home to the needy of our city, or paid their rent herself', remarked Pauline crossly. 'All she did was not hassle them for payment when really she should have made a bit of an effort. If people think they can get away with things they will. What do you reckon? You know her.'

'I think she is very sincere in wanting to help people. The board of management didn't make any fuss about her not collecting all the rent for ages. Then suddenly it became the big issue. When she drove up in a new car, I think. They worked out she couldn't afford one on what they were paying her.'

'And she could explain the new car?'

'I suppose so. It was none of our business. Just because a person acquires an expensive new toy you don't assume he or she has been embezzling money. People are too ready to jump to conclusions. What's for tea?'

Pauline had forgotten it was her turn to cook. How she could forget when she had to cook every second night was beyond Eileen, but often forget she did. The vegetarian phase was mercifully past. Now it was scrounging in the cupboards to see if there were enough ingredients to make a pasta sauce, only to discover there was no pasta. In the end they had scrambled eggs and chips — again. Eileen tried not to mind. Food was only a means of survival, not the high point of each day. But if God hadn't meant us to enjoy our food, why was there such a wonderful variety?

The Crown case against Irene faltered. People rang up talkback radio programs expressing their disgust that a women who had genuinely tried to help people was being persecuted by the government.

Fiona and Sarah changed sides.

Mandy stuck to her guns. No amount of hyperbole would convince her.

The trial attracted more and more spectators, who tried the judge's patience sorely. He was more at home with civil matters. Crime, and particularly a crime which attracted media attention, was not his cup of tea.

Pauline's religion class did a project on social justice, using Irene's case as the main discussion point. 'We must make it as relevant as possible. Religion should not be an extra to our lives', Pauline explained to a sceptical parent. She invited Eileen to speak to her class, to tell them all she knew about the case, and was miffed when Eileen refused. She tried to organise a trip to the courts with her students, to view proceedings, but by the time she had cleared a day with other teachers and had the consent forms printed the case was finished.

The court was packed with reporters for the judge's final summing up. He began to enjoy the attention, pleased that the pencil sketch shown of him on television was a flattering likeness.

He strongly intimated that this case should never have come before his court. While the defendant's skills in bookkeeping may have been a trifle wanting, it was clear that she was a competent and compassionate social worker, in which capacity she had been employed. It may be that the honorary treasurer would need to look to her own performance in the future. The jury, properly directed by the judge, felt they had little choice. They stayed out long enough to get a free lunch, then returned a not guilty verdict. Irene smiled her relief. It had been a trying few months. Her solicitor had already begun claims for compensation for unlawful dismissal, and the Salvation Army had offered her a position overseeing their youth shelters. She could afford to nod distantly at Fiona and Sarah. Richard she cut dead. He'd had to be subpoenaed.

The media succumbed to self-congratulation and moved on to a new outrage.

Having prayed for justice, Eileen was delighted that the result accorded with her views. Heaven wasn't always so accommodating. Tom was back, so she didn't have the worry of running the parish any longer. She could concentrate on the new catechumen group, meeting each week to inquire into the teachings of the Catholic Church. In the good old days it was called 'taking instruction'. It never occurred to the hierarchy then that a person might learn about the teachings of the One Holy Catholic and Apostolic Church and not wish to become a member. Whether they would be accepted as a member was another thing, although numbers were needed to combat heresy. It wouldn't do to let the proddies get ahead!

Nowadays it was all so different. People went on a 'faith journey'. Members of the parish community joined the group as sponsors, willing to share their faith experience with the newcomer, helping them to decide if the Catholic Church was for them. Although Eileen enjoyed running this program, she did wonder if it had a higher degree of warm fuzzies than doctrinal content. Many of the people who signed up ended up being received into the church, and those who didn't left with no ill feelings. It was one of the few times she felt that she grew close to people, although once the program was finished the participants went their various ways. After that it was a friendly smile at mass, a warm greeting at Christmas, a special plea to be remembered in her prayers when something was going wrong in their lives. They were ready to share misfortunes. Good times they kept for themselves.

This year's bunch was a motley crew. Single parents, unemployable teenagers, and a middle-of-the-road middle-aged couple. They never seemed to get the high-flyers. 'Of such is the kingdom, the kingdom of heaven', she hummed to herself at the end of the first meeting for the year. By next Easter they would be ready for reception into the church during the Easter vigil ceremony. Sister Josephine was probably beaming down at her from heaven as she went about harvesting souls. At school it had all seemed so obvious. The Catholic Church was the right way. All the others were wrong. Misguided, sincere, but wrong. She would go about like a little missionary and explain to people, who, immediately convinced, would change their religion and join the One True Church.

She had hardly had time to learn it didn't work like that when she joined the convent. The members of the tennis club exhibited greater concern for their backhands and first serves than thirsting for the truth. Being non-religious also had some advantages. They could stay out late on Saturday nights, eat supper well after midnight with no worry about fasting, and sleep in on Sunday morning. Luxury unknown in Eileen's household. Her parents always went to early mass, and Eileen found if she went to any mass later than nine o'clock her stomach rumbled and she felt weak from hunger. She couldn't have even a cup of tea if she wanted to receive communion, and going to mass without receiving the sacrament seemed a bit of a waste. Clare, as a university student, started to develop 'sloppy habits', as her mother disapprovingly called them, just making the eleven o'clock mass by the last possible minute.

Clare and Lilian often called in on a Sunday night after tea. The four of them would sit in the little living room, sometimes watching television, but often just chatting. Pauline became twittery when they were there, talking too loudly about things that happened at school and rattling the tea cups while she prepared supper.

Clare's hair was now back to its natural auburn, cut in a severe boyish style. Lilian had beautiful hair, which she looped and tied at the back of her head, tiny curls escaping about the nape of her neck. Soft waves framed her smooth-skinned face. Like Maud Gonne, Eileen thought, not Brangwen. Men would write poetry for her.

She ran her hand through her own thin, greying hair, cropped for convenience. No permanent waves for Eileen. The gesture made her think of the furore in the convent when one of the nuns had started putting her hair into rollers every night. That rated a letter to Mother Provincial. Not wearing a veil was one thing, but curlers! John XXIII had much to answer for.

The feeling when Mother Eleanor had cut her hair right off came back to her. She had worn her hair long for years, in plaits at school, and in a ponytail on the weekends. Now it was all on the floor around her chair and she looked perfectly hideous. Thank goodness they were not allowed mirrors so she wouldn't have to look at her ugliness. She offered it up for all her sins of vanity, but her heart wasn't in it. It wasn't really vain to like the feel of long hair, or the look of it if it suited you. In her heart of hearts she knew that it was. Hating to have her hair cut showed that she did not love God enough. St Clare of Assisi had rejoiced when her hair had been cropped, kneeling in a sunlit glade while St Francis hacked at her golden locks with a pair of blunt scissors, shedding all pretentions to womanly beauty so that she could be totally dedicated to God. That was how the *Stories of the Saints* described it, and the young Eileen never doubted its authority.

Short hair suited her sister Clare. Eileen felt hers was frumpish, but she honestly didn't mind. It was preferable to having to spend time or money on trying to maintain a style. Pauline was lucky. Her hair was naturally curly.

Lilian waved white, long-fingered hands in the air as she talked. Clare sat on the floor leaning against Lilian's legs, warming herself from the glow of the electric heater. Lilian gently massaged Clare's shoulders. Pauline stared, stopped twittering for long enough to say she had lots of corrections to do and would they excuse her, and hurried to her room. Sounds of flute offstage. Lilian gave no indication that she noticed anything amiss. Eileen wished someone would massage her shoulders. She was bored with her yoga asanas. Her bedroom floor was cold in the morning. Meditation time dragged. Her spiritual life needed an injection of funds, but she knew of no donor except the Source and she didn't seem able to tap into that at the moment. Lilian and Clare looked very content together. She was glad Clare was now happy.

Her days were busy, but time seemed to drag. She had not expected to miss Mrs Cameron as much as she did, but now she realised that she had gained as much from visiting the old lady as ever she had given. She missed Amber-Mae. Would she one day open the front door and find her, beaming face upturned expectantly, on the doorstep? In a perverse way she even missed Karen's whinging. Eileen acknowledged that she wasn't close to any person. There were barriers between her and Clare. She loved her parents but they had each other. Pauline was always busy too. There wasn't a time of day when they could sit down and talk calmly about their doings. Not as she imagined married couples did. Being married meant that someone cared most about you.

Having children meant that you cared most for them. Children went out into the world but you still had that bond. There was no person who put Eileen first.

Her mind told her that she shouldn't care about that. She was the servant of the Lord. But her heart told her that she would love to sit down and have someone massage her shoulders.

Power walking took the place of yoga. Pauline's suggestion. Eileen found her back was a bit sore, and headstands were not recommended for the time being. Power walking meant you bustled about the block and peered into other people's gardens. Dogs barked at you. Other power walkers greeted. Runners passed you with barely disguised scorn. You breathed in air which you hoped was fresh and unpolluted. Eileen enjoyed it. Minnie thoroughly approved and had no trouble keeping up.

Clare predicted that Karen would return, and she was right. A few weeks after she had left, she rang up to tell Eileen she was back and to ask if Eileen knew of somewhere to live. She was staying with a girlfriend, but it was a bit cramped because her girlfriend had three children, and she had two, and that Jimmy was a selfish pig and she should have listened to Sister in the first place. Eileen had never said a word against Jimmy, but she understood that her body language had spoken — loud and clear.

This was surely a case for the Relief Housing Scheme. A chance for Doreen. Eileen rang her immediately and left a message on her answering machine. Doreen got back to her two days later, informing her that all the emergency houses were occupied, but promising to see what she could do. A week passed. Karen rang her daily, sounding more and more desperate. Her phone calls were always soundtracked by screaming children. Eileen thought Karen lined them all up and orchestrated them to the correct pitch before she dialled her number.

One of them would have cracked if she hadn't run into Irene and mentioned the problem to her. 'Leave it with me. It's not quite homeless youth, but I am sure that we can help out. It must be murder for them in that tiny house with all those kids. No wonder kids get bashed. There's a limit to how much any person can take.'

Eileen worried all day. There seemed to be this constant threat of violence hanging over Amber-Mae, and she couldn't bear it. The little girl had so much good in her, so much potential.

Irene telephoned that night. She had found a house where the rent could be subsidised, two streets away from Eileen and Pauline. Karen, Amber-Mae and Aaron would now be neighbours. She could wave at them as she powered her way past each evening.

She drew the line at helping Karen move, but she dropped by the next day to see how they were settling in. The house was not in the expected Karen muddle. Karen had never got over her tidy phase. She hadn't become really fat again either, so Clare's reform program had done her some good.

Amber-Mae proudly showed Eileen her room with her toys lined up against the wall. She still had the doll Eileen had given her last Christmas and a holy picture Eileen had given her just before she went away. That was pinned on the wall next to her bed.

'Do you say your prayers every day, Amber-Mae?' she asked.

'Yes, prayers', Amber-Mae assented, although to what she was assenting Eileen was not sure. Now that the little girl lived just around the corner she could teach her about God. No person deserved to grow up without the knowledge of God.

Praying in the morning and walking at night fell into routine. She had tried praying as she walked, but there were too many distractions. Eileen liked to inspect the gardens and smile at people sitting on their verandahs. She went a different route each night so as not to get in a rut, although there was a limit to the number of variations she could find when she always started and ended at the same spot. Mostly her homeward journey took her past Karen's house, where Amber-Mae would be hanging over the gate waiting for her.

'Hello, Sister Eileen. I've got this for you.'

'This' would be a flower, occasionally a soursob, which Amber-Mae held aloft, confident of a favourable response. Eileen would take the proffered gift as though it were a precious gem and thank Amber-Mae.

'What have you been doing today?' she would ask, and Amber-Mae would tell her. Minnie would sniff about impatiently, wanting to continue around the corner to her comfortable mat, where she could rest her legs. She was not getting any younger.

Who would have thought such an innocent routine could lead to tragedy? In the early evening light Eileen powered around the corner. Amber-Mae was not hanging over the gate, but had climbed over the fence and was starting to cross the road to meet her. Eileen sensed rather than saw the car and broke into a run to prevent the child from crossing the road. Minnie picked up speed and set off after her, looking to neither right nor left.

There was a squeal of brakes and a thud. Minnie's broken body rolled to the kerb. The car sped on.

Eileen rushed across, forgetting Amber-Mae in her distress. Minnie was alive, but only just. She was obviously suffering great pain. Instinctively Eileen picked her up by the hind legs and bashed her head against the concrete gutter, putting her out of her misery. Only when Amber-Mae began to scream did she remember that she was there, watching. Eileen put Minnie's body down and reached out for Amber-Mae, but the little girl backed away from her, still staring in horror at Minnie's now lifeless body.

It had all happened so quickly Eileen had had no time to think. Now, sitting on the side of the gutter, her legs weak and trembling, she felt sick.

Minnie's spirit had left her. There seemed little connection between the battered, broken, hairy mass at her feet and the cheerful dog which had been running beside her a few minutes before. No doubt Minnie was with Mrs Cameron now. Animals mightn't go to heaven, but there was no way Mrs C would allow Minnie to be anywhere else but with her.

Amber-Mae had quietened down too. She walked hesitantly over to Eileen, looked at Minnie, and touched her body. She said nothing, just looked at Eileen.

'Minnie's dead', Eileen said. 'She was in pain and I helped her to die quickly. Now she is at peace.'

There was no reply.

'You see how careful we have to be on the roads', Eileen said then. 'A car can run over you so easily, and it doesn't even have to stop. You must never run on the road.'

'Amber-Mae, where are you? Gawd, what are you doing out there? Come back inside at once.' Karen's voice shrilled across their gloom. She came out of the house and saw.

'Gawd, poor little mite. Them drivers! Didn't even stop, the brute! Typical! Poor little thing.'

Karen picked up the body with great tenderness.

'Come inside and have a coffee. Things like that can shake you up. Come on Amber-Mae, bring Sister Eileen in for a drink.'

The funeral procession went up the front path and around the back of the house. Karen put Minnie down at the back step. She went inside, put the kettle on, and then returned, found the spade, and dug a hole in the soft earth near the fence. Placing Minnie's body in the hole, she covered it with earth. Then they went inside for coffee.

While they drank the warming liquid, Karen made a little cardboard plaque: Here lies Minnie, dearly loved dog of Mrs C and

Sister Eileen. 'That's what we used to do with our pets when I was little', she explained, as she attached the plaque to a stick and put it at the head of the grave. 'We had lots of cats and dogs, one way and another.'

Eileen had never imagined Karen as a young child. She thought she had been born fat and fourteen.

Amber-Mae stuck a flower at the other end of the grave, as she had seen them do on television. She didn't seem to be suffering any after-effects.

Eileen thanked Karen sincerely, and walked home, sadly conscious that there was no longer a little black figure at her heels.

Pauline was most upset to hear of Minnie's demise. Far more upset than she had been over Mrs Cameron, it seemed to Eileen. Strange that; she hadn't even wanted the dog in the first place. Eileen wondered if they should get a cat.

She wouldn't have minded if life didn't seem just more and more of the same. The outer framework never changed. There were variations within the outer structure, but it boiled down to meetings, hospital visits, taking the children for first comunion and confirmation, supervising the catechists and the catechumens, and a few parish visits when she had time. It wasn't enough. She needed something to hold on to. Someone to hold on to, Clare would have said, if she had known of Eileen's anguish.

Her mother sensed that something was wrong. 'You never really got over that cold you had all those months ago. Perhaps you need a holiday. Time to regain your strength. You're not getting any younger, you know.'

Thanks, Mum, that's all I need. Reminder of impending mortality when I haven't done anything to justify my time here. Had she achieved sainthood all would have been well. Having to make do with lesser successes, there was a limit below which one could not go without feeling profound dissatisfaction.

Eileen's mother rang her one morning to tell her that her father had had what the doctor thought could have been a slight stroke. 'He was supposed to go into hospital for a few days observation and tests but he refused. You know your father. Says he'd rather stay at home and be observed here. He just keeled over and couldn't speak for a bit. He seems much better now, but it's a worry.'

Visiting him that evening, she found him sitting up in bed with a book balanced on his knees and a tray with the remains of afternoon tea next to his bed. He looked thin, tired, more lined, but he smiled cheerily. 'Took me seventy-eight years to work out how to do it. Your mother's been fussing over me like an old chook. She's even wheeled the television in so I can watch the golf. Clare's been to see me this afternoon, and now you are here. How's the world treating you?'

Eileen sensed that he didn't want to talk about his 'turn'. Her father was so rarely ill that he didn't know how to cope with it when he was. The only reference he made was: 'Wanted to put me into hospital but I didn't fancy trying to sleep in a room with a lot of old men who snored'.

'They might have given you a private room, Dad, with television and a bell to ring when you wanted attention', Eileen replied.

'Well, if you can find me a bell I've got all that here, and your mother's as good as any nurse', he said.

Eileen's mother said she didn't fancy running up and down the hallway to the sound of a bell. Eileen noticed that she looked quite worn out, and wondered if she mightn't be the one ending up in hospital. Her parents worried a lot about being parted, either by sickness or death.

'How's Anne getting on? Still overseas?' her father asked.

'Last we heard she was in Rome. There was some talk about her going to Lebanon, but I think she decided that was too dangerous. She didn't want to end up living in a wardrobe. She's studying early Bible history. Anne always seems to study and never do anything with it. When the Lebanon idea fell through, she wrote that she was thinking about India or Egypt.'

'Where does she get her money from, to go tripping around the world?' asked her mother.

'She had a legacy from her aunt, and her professor has helped out with accommodation. Anne lives frugally, so she'd manage.'

Did live frugally, she thought to herself, remembering the new clothes. Goodness knows what needs she has acquired since she left the order.

Pauline was sympathetic about her father. 'It's the beginning of the end. That's what happened to my mother. Right as rain one day, had a bad fall which really knocked her around, and she was never the same. Old people don't get over things easily.'

Thanks, Pauline. Just the sort of thing I wanted to hear. Go and play your flute, or write your caustic comments on the bottom of some poor unsuspecting student's essay.

When they were sure that her father was making good progress, in fact seemed back to normal, Clare and Lilian booked an overseas trip. Ted offered to look after the children for a month.

'God help them, or him. I'm not quite sure who is going to need it', said Clare. ' But I think it's time for me to live my own life a bit more. Otherwise I'll miss out altogether. Lilian is going to show me Paris.'

Eileen had always wanted to see Paris, to visit the art galleries and see the fabulous fashions in the dress designers' windows. She knew that she could walk the length and breadth of Paris and never grow tired.

Chapter Fourteen

It was a few days later that her father asked her an unusual question. 'When your mother and I die you get half our money. What will you do with it?'

'Nothing. I've taken a vow of poverty. I'd give it to the order and they'd probably use it for the missions. We're always short of money there.'

'Well, what if we bought you a ticket to go overseas, and gave you some money for living expenses. They couldn't give that to the missions. Surely you're entitled to holidays the same as everyone else', said her father. Her mother sat next to him on the bed. The pair of them were beaming, having conceived this wonderful plan through hours of discussion, now anticipating her delight.

Eileen's face went quite pink, and she felt tears pricking her eyes. What lovely people her parents were. Now she could go overseas. She didn't have to be the one to miss out.

'I could visit Anne, and spend some of the time with Clare and Lilian', she said. 'Let me think about it and see if I can be allowed time off. I work for the parish, remember.'

The joy and excitement subsided, replaced by unease. It was a lot of money they were offering. She shouldn't really just take off, wandering the world at her pleasure. That wasn't what she was supposed to be doing. It would be different if she went overseas to study, but just to jaunt around for a month — that sounded like self-indulgence. What would Mother Eleanor have said to the notion of one of her novices indulging herself for a month!

She talked over the idea with Pauline, who understood her wish to bring some change into her life. In fact, Pauline admitted to feeling restless at school. There was a limit, and she had reached hers. The provincial was keen on the idea of Pauline running the big two-storey house in the city which had been set up to provide shelter for homeless girls. That would leave a vacancy at school. Why didn't Eileen go back to teaching for a while? That would be a change from administering the parish. Somewhere in the discussion Pauline had forgotten about the idea of her going overseas. Eileen took that to indicate that she didn't think it was suitable. I bet she'd be off like a shot if she had the chance, Eileen thought. No wonder we share bad news more easily than good news. People find it far easier to sympathise than rejoice in your good fortune. And why hadn't she been approached about the shelter for homeless girls? Surely that was more her style than Pauline's.

Go back to teaching? No thanks! Quite a few years since she had trod that path and she was quite sure that she didn't want to again.

Anne had escaped completely from the drudgery of the classroom, but she had had the sense to see that she was temperamentally unfit for the task. Her sense of survival was strong, even then.

Eileen had initially enjoyed the contact with the girls. They treated her like minor royalty, because she was that phenomenon: a young nun. They crowded about her in the playground, stealing threads from her veil and asking all sorts of questions. She soon learnt the necessary reserve. It was amazing how an innocent comment could be used against you.

The classes were all big, the preparation time consuming, and corrections a horrendous burden. On top of that there was tennis coaching, the Young Catholic Students meetings, and the Children of Mary, who might look lovely in their blue cloaks and white veils but who still needed to be instructed and rostered. Most nights she collapsed on her bed and was asleep within a few minutes. Even her youth and energy were taxed.

She'd been put to work as soon as the degree was completed. The luxury of teacher training came later. A degree, goodwill, and the help of God was all that was considered necessary. Considering the standard of education most of the teaching nuns had acquired in those days, God must have been very busy. When Eileen found out the true situation, she wondered how she and her fellow students ever managed to matriculate. The good nuns, in setting up their schools, put far greater reliance on hard work than hard study. Perhaps she was being unfair. Higher study was a luxury they simply couldn't afford, and the hierarchy, all male, weren't prepared to make it possible for them. Hierarchy became more pragmatic in line with government directives. She knew that if she hadn't won a scholarship, and if the bishop hadn't put pressure on the teaching nuns to upgrade their qualifications, there was no way she would have gone to university.

She began her teaching career — even before she had finished studying — in fear and trepidation, feeling totally inadequate. Reverend Mother Agnes had run the school as her little empire. Young nuns trembled and obeyed. Things didn't change until the supply of young nuns dried up, and lay staff had to be employed.

She remembered their first lay teacher, a married woman with two young children. Mother Agnes was concerned that, by employing her, they were taking her away from her rightful place in the home. She soothed her conscience with the knowledge that Mrs Evans had approached them for a position, not the other way around.

Mrs Evans was not allowed to join them for morning tea or lunch. The nuns couldn't eat in front of her, so she didn't spend recess and lunchtime with them. One of the students used to carry a tray bearing a cup of tea and biscuits from the convent kitchen, across the courtyard, to the tiny office where Mrs Evans sat. If she felt lonely she never said so.

Teaching in those days meant big classes. Ninety in her religion class, because for that they combined two forms. Mrs Evans could not be trusted with the teaching of religion.

There was a certain impersonality in imparting God's truth to ninety children at a time. Still, Jesus had preached to thousands in one go and had managed to get his message across.

Despite the size of the class, discipline wasn't really a problem. The girls were somewhat in awe of her habit. Besides, with that number, she soon learnt to have a formal, structured approach to a lesson. There was no way one could be jocular and keep order.

Mrs Evans, judging from the sounds in the room where she taught, did have problems with discipline. Much laughter, not all of it discreet. And she had funny ideas about using drama as a teaching method. Too often her class was out in the sun, brandishing sticks for swords, following Joan of Arc to beat the English.

Eileen smiled to herself, remembering the pet show. This was to raise money for the missions. While a tidy sum of money was collected, and the girls had a wonderful time during the lunchbreak parading their pets and receiving prizes, for the rest of the day classrooms were chaos. The principal went about with her mouth in a very thin line.

Mrs Evans had supplied the ribbon out of her own money and Eileen had designed and made a number of rosettes for prizes. In so doing she became implicated in the whole 'fiasco', as Mother Agnes called it. The memory of the girls' animated faces faded long before that of messes in the classroom and distractions from wandering kittens and an escaped mouse. Mrs Evans's organisational abilities had not stretched to planning holding pens for the pets during class time. At the end of the year she left because she was pregnant. Mother Julian sighed with relief and rearranged the timetable, hoping to be spared the necessity of employing outsiders ever again. However, the wall had been breached, and she was forced to employ two lay teachers the following year, one of them a man. What was worse, he drove a red sports car, which he parked under the tree in the schoolyard. The girls thought he was wonderful. He left after a complaint from a parent.

No, she had never wanted to be a teacher! Once she entered the convent it was either that or being a nurse. Being a nurse apppealed even less.

Looking back, she realised that she had been silly to join a teaching order.

Half her school friends trained to be teachers. Few girls branched into interesting professions in those days. Only one had got in to Medicine and another had studied Law, but they were the exceptions. A good many trained as nurses, some went into banks or the public service, and the rest became teachers. There was always work for teachers; the baby boomers saw to that. For most of them their job was just something to fill in time until the babies arrived.

Her degree finished, Eileen assumed she would stay teaching at her old school, but Mother Agnes called her into her office. 'Sister, we are sending you to Star of the Sea Girls School in Geppsdale. Mother Julian has been principal there for a number of years. I think she could do with some help. You leave on Friday's train. I have made arrangements for you to do your Diploma of Education by correspondence.'

Just like that. Parcelled off. Leaving in three days. Rebellion. Frustration. Her university graduate status meant nothing in the eyes of the order. To them she was a young nun to go where she was sent. She didn't bother discussing with anyone the anguish she felt at leaving her familiar surroundings and the other sisters. Self was to be denied.

Eileen felt tears pricking her eyelids as she packed her belongings the night before she left, but she refused to give in to them. At recreation time the nuns had a farewell concert and party. Pauline played her flute, and Anne, quite brave in familiar company, made a speech and presented her with a book on educational theory that she had particularly wanted. She looked at them all. Some she would miss not at all, but it would be a wrench to leave Mother Eleanor, Sister Celine, and even Anne, whom she had come to appreciate through their years of novitiate and university study together. Sister Celine gave her a small cloth bag which contained a number of daffodil bulbs. 'You'll know the right time to plant them, and when they bloom you can think of us all back here.'

It was then she had to fight hardest to control her tears.

She had known the order had a school at Geppsdale, but that was all. Her father told her it was a large country town, a centre for dairy farms and timber mills. Friendly people, as patient as the cows which queued up each morning and evening to be relieved of their milk. Innovation and radical ideas had found no sanctuary in Geppsdale, although once the local farmers had driven to parliament house and poured litres of milk down the stone steps. Politicians found it a very slippery path until they restored the milk subsidy. The revolution now over, tradition prevailed.

As she sat in the train that was taking her to her new life, she tried to cheer herself up. Living in the country meant living with nature in all its splendour. She would renew her joy in God's creation. Country people were simple, salt of the earth types. No doubt true goodness and virtue were to be found in every country cottage wreathed in climbing roses and jasmine. The dilapidated weatherboard farmhouses at Geppsdale bore no resemblance to her fanciful picture, but by the time she had visited any of them she had adjusted her ideas somewhat.

At Geppsdale station Mother Julian was waiting for her, ready to drive her to the convent in their Holden. She greeted Eileen with a kiss on both cheeks, picked up her one suitcase, and walked to the car. 'Welcome to Star of the Sea. We are looking forward to having a new teacher.'

Was there a hint of a sneer in the way she pronounced 'new', as in 'don't think you are coming here straight from the city and the university to tell us how to do what we have been doing very well for the last twelve years'?

Geppsdale had a long wide main street, in which some of the buildings had retained their verandahs and wrought iron. The street was lined with trees, and the overall effect was one of sleepy charm. Eileen felt her spirits lift. Then they turned into another street. She saw the convent and school. Her spirits plummeted. They were ugly. Eileen saw the fibro buildings planted seemingly at random around a red-brick block which was the main part of the school. The convent was a weatherboard house next to the church. She tried not to think of the gracious bluestone building, with its beautiful chapel and restful cloister, that she had left behind.

The convent was barely adequate. Eileen learnt that an earlier parish priest had refused to live in it, so the bishop had solved the problem by building a new presbytery and making the old house available to the nuns, who were invited to set up a school in the diocese. It had enough rooms for the five nuns, but they were poky; hot in summer and freezing in winter. The kitchen was ill-equipped, with a wood stove which provided more smoke than heat, and insufficient cupboard space. The laundry also left much to be desired. Until one of the parishioners had handed on a second-hand washing machine, they had had to do their washing in a copper and two troughs. Sister Regina, who was in charge of housekeeping, felt that she was serving her time in purgatory here on earth. Dipping her hands in and out of cold water had not helped her chilblains. It was too easy for the other nuns to regard her as a servant, complaining if the food tasted smoky (which it often did due to the condition of the stove), and expressing dissatisfaction if their clothes were not always ironed correctly.

On Saturdays they all joined in with the cleaning. In convents all over Australia, on any Saturday morning, there were nuns busy with their housework.

Sister Celine would not have approved of the garden. Sister Regina certainly didn't have time to worry about it. None of the other nuns showed much interest, and, after a few attempts to dig the dry, claggy earth, Eileen could see why. She persevered, making a compost heap, which she used to soften the soil, built up two garden beds (she needed one for her daffodil bulbs), and encouraged grass to grow on the rest. There was one tree which gave shade to the front of the house, and she decided to grow a creeper which would twine around the trunk of the tree.

Sister Regina was thrilled with it all, especially the pots of parsley and mint growing at the back door. Mother Julian had a tendency to sniff when she saw Eileen working in the garden, a sniff which said: 'Have you nothing better to do with your time? I hope your work program is up to date, corrections done, and all your lessons prepared. However, I would not like to bet on it.'

Eileen had no intention of giving up her gardening. Without it she believed that she would go completely mad. It was her outlet, her link with the place she had left. When the daffodils bloomed, she picked them and put them in a vase in front of Our Lady's statue in the church. Sister Celine would have approved of that.

At Geppsdale there were five nuns in all. Mother Julian was the principal of the school as well as being their Reverend Mother. A woman who had made a virtue of repression.

Sister Jacinta was next in command. She had a look of permanent disapproval — or was it discontent — stamped on her face. Eileen found both her superiors hard to talk to. If she talked about any new idea for the school, they thought she was criticising them and became very defensive. If she went ahead with any change, however minor, she was criticised for not discussing it with them first. What made it particularly difficult was the fact that she didn't think much of either of them as teachers. If you counted silence in the classroom as the measure of success, then they would both rate highly, but, while Mother Julian had the occasional spark, Sister Jacinta's lessons were all characterised by stultifying boredom. The energy emanating from Eileen's classroom was an affront to both of them.

Sister Regina certainly loved a chat. She was always ready with a warmed teapot when she heard the final bell signalling the school dismissal for the day. Eileen loved to sit in the cosy kitchen, drinking tea and talking about the old convent. Sister Regina had been a novice with Sister Celine and knew nearly all the nuns of the order. She talked nostalgically of the old days, a nostalgia which Eileen shared. Sometimes Sister Regina became weepy, although never in front of the other nuns. Eileen tried to help her by hanging out the washing and cleaning the bathroom, until Mother Julian called her to one side and said that that was not her work. She was to concentrate on her teaching — and the garden, if she must. Sister Regina was in charge of the housekeeping, and that was her job. She seemed to have no awareness that the poor old thing, plagued by rheumatism and chilblains, was simply worn out. The demands made by the uncomfortable convent were too great.

The other two nuns, Sister Theodore and Sister Gerard, had been novices together, had taught together for many years, and relied upon each other for most things. Clare, when she met them, thought them enchanting, and called them 'the bookends' and said they were 'too cute'. But she didn't have to live with them or teach in the same school with them. When she first met them, Eileen had thought that they were real sisters, they looked so alike. Sister Regina told her that they were really good friends who had grown to resemble each other. 'Like people and their pet dogs', she said. 'Have you ever noticed how people come to look like their pets?'

This was over an after-school cup of tea. Sister Regina wriggled her rear more comfortably on the hard-backed chair as she went on with the story. 'Gerard, she entered later than most of us. Invalid mother, or something like that. Theodore entered at the same time, but she was about ten years younger, a timid little thing in those days. Hardly said a word throughout her entire novitiate. We wondered if she had something wrong with her tongue. Gerard sort of took her under her wing. She seemed to cry such a lot in those days. The novice mistress used to be quite sharp with her, tell her that there was no place for waterworks in the convent. One time Gerard stood up for her and there was no end of fuss. We thought the two of them might be asked to leave.'

Sister Theodore dissolving in tears! Eileen couldn't imagine it. Obviously the order had toughened her over the years.

Mother Julian walked into the kitchen at this point, looking meaningfully at the cups of tea and the comradely stance of the two drinking them. Sister Regina jumped up, taking the cups over to the sink.

'Would you like a cup of tea, Mother?' she asked Mother Julian.

'No thank you. I shall wait until the evening meal. It will be ready by six?'

It was always ready by six. Their day followed a rigid routine. Mother Julian saw to that. Eileen could see some virtue in a strict regime. It meant things got done, and you always knew where you were supposed to be at a set time. Her life was still ruled by bells at school and inaudible bells in the convent. Religious orders all over the world were reassessing their lifestyles and allowing the winds of change to blow freely. Not in Mother Julian's sphere of influence. Change, if it were to come, must come slowly — so slowly that it would not disturb her life.

Eileen took more notice of Sisters Theodore and Gerard after Regina had told her about them. Now it seemed that Theodore was the strong one, protecting Gerard. Not that there was much to protect her from. Mother Julian and Sister Jacinta tended to leave them alone. At recreation time they would smile at Eileen but never sit with her. Instead they retired to their two armchairs by the window, where they talked softly together, knitting and sewing, watching what little life there was in Geppsdale go past the window. The girls they taught thought they had second sight, but the only extra sight they had was through the lacy curtain.

Eileen, being in her twenties thought they were quite old, but Sister Gerard was in her late fifties, and Theodore ten years younger. They had been sent out to teach with a level of education only slightly higher than the classes they taught. Their students excelled in neat handwriting and a knowledge of etiquette.

Sister Jacinta had said: 'Experience essential, university study a waste of time', but Eileen couldn't agree with her.

The school catered for the daughters of the less wealthy farmers. Rich girls went to boarding school in the city. During the holidays they sat about in smart circles in the milk bar hoping to attract the attention of the rich young boys who also went to boarding school in the city. Eileen could always pick them by a peculiarly haughty expression, a languor which exile had imposed.

Girls from Star of the Sea worked in the milk bar.

The first year was hard. She learnt a lot about teaching and a lot about herself. Where was this patience so carefully encouraged by Mother Eleanor? She was homesick, but not for her family as she used to be. Both Pauline and Anne wrote to her, and she longed for their letters, with news of the old convent and school. They were becoming caught up with Vatican II and all its implications for their order. Eileen felt out of things.

Mother Julian was diagnosed as having a weak heart. The doctors ordered her complete rest or they couldn't answer for the consequences. She had no idea of resting and went off to the missions, where she lived until a ripe old age. So much for doctors!

In consequence, Eileen was made principal only two years after she had finished the Diploma of Education. Promotion sweetened her exile. Life became more interesting.

Sister Jacinta was her embittered and disappointed deputy, whose self-appointed task was to curb Eileen's youthful excesses. Sister Regina continued to keep house for them, but was becoming more and more forgetful.

Eileen's strengths were in education policy and staff rapport, not in administration. Sister Jacinta couldn't get on with anyone and was an uninspiring teacher, but she loved administration. Drawing up timetables, organising the school calender, keeping track of the staff absences, and arranging substitute teachers put her in a frenzy of bustling delight. She would have been given two out of ten for communication skills, but that actually worked for her. The staff were too scared of her acid tongue to argue very much, and the girls straightened their stockings and pulled down their tunics to the regulation length at the mere hint of her footsteps. Eileen was left free to soothe ruffled feelings and revitalise the education side of the school.

She set forth on a reform program guided by limited experience, lecture notes from her Diploma of Education, and a burning zeal to establish high standards of excellence within a caring framework, where the needs of the individual students were completely met and each realised her full potential. This was the formula outlined by her tertiary lecturers who forgot to also mention that it was unattainable.

Sisters Theodore and Gerard had no place in her grand plan, but removing them required tact and delicacy. She squandered many a meditation period over the best way to go about it. How do you tell two old dears who have dedicated their lives to teaching that they are underqualified and too old-fashioned? Retrench? No. Retrain? What a brilliant idea! Why not recommend that they go to the Geppsdale Adult and Further Education College to do a refresher course in teaching junior secondary mathematics? Their fears about this massive jolt to their daily routine were soothed by assuring them that this was what the bishop wanted. Well, he would have if he knew what was best for the school. Even more importantly, she had the approval of Reverend Mother Provincial, so poor old Theodore and Gerard didn't stand a chance.

They reacted negatively. Sister Theodore refused to speak to her at breakfast, which was preferable to Sister Gerard's exaggerated politeness. 'Don't worry about it, they'll get over it', said Sister Regina when they were alone in the kitchen. But Eileen wasn't worrying about it. She felt strong.

At first they set off each morning full of resentment, sandwiches housed in their cases next to notebook and pen. It took a month to turn them into seasoned students. By then they no longer spent recreation time in knitting and gossiping; they were too busy doing their assignments. Strictly speaking this wasn't recreation, but none of the others could bring herself to object.

In the meantime Eileen replaced them with lay staff who were young, well qualified, dymanic, and totally 'with it'. Sister Jacinta was alarmed when she hinted that they might also have to ask Mrs Clements and Mrs Harvey to retire. 'Impossible idea. Mrs Harvey taught needlework to mothers of half these girls. Parents respect her. Mrs Clements, a good Catholic', she barked at Eileen, then strode out of the room before Eileen could ask her what being a good Catholic had to do with teaching geography.

So the two old teachers were reprieved. Eileen wasn't sure she could replace them anyway. Her advertisement for three new teachers to deal with art, maths and science, and French and history didn't provoke a flood of applicants. Geppsdale wasn't every young teacher's dream placement.

'It's always darkest before the dawn', Sister Regina counselled, when she confided her fears that they would start the year without sufficient staff. 'It'll work out in time, you'll see. I'll say a prayer to St Joseph of Cupertino.'

As Regina had predicted, he came up trumps. With a few lucky arrivals in the district and one not totally ethical poach from the local high school, Eileen had her staff ready for the new school year.

To Mrs Clements and Mrs Harvey she had added Mrs Branigan (art), Miss Blackford (French and history), Mrs McGee (maths and science). Eileen would teach senior English and religion. Sister Jacinta would look after junior English and religion (heaven help them!) as well as being in charge of the library.

Presiding over her first staff meeting, aglow with the desire to make her mark, she felt challenged. Star of the Sea would become the best school in Geppsdale. Mother Eleanor would have warned her about pride had she been there.

The younger staff were all for developing potential and individuality in their students. They didn't advocate a negotiated curriculum because this was still to come, but new maths, new social studies, new English, and even new religion were all the go.

Sister Jacinta said that Jennifer Branigan's skirts were too short and her hair teased too high, but the art students loved her. When they started taking off all the prizes at the local show, Jacinta modified her criticism a little. 'Artistic temperament. Make allowances. Not good example for girls though', she said, as the news of yet more prizes came their way.

Eileen, concerned for staff unity, organised a short meeting each morning in the staffroom. She went through any change to the order of the day, and occasionally gave short pep talks. Stirrings from the feminist movement had even reached the cloisters. 'It is imperative that the girls be educated thoroughly. They should be as well equipped as their brothers to cope with the modern world', she said one morning. 'That is one of the reasons our order was founded.' She could see by the looks on all their faces that the intentions of their founder was not the guiding principle of the lay staff.

'Waste of time', protested Mrs Harvey. 'Most of the girls will be married five years after they leave school. Needlework is more important for them than geometry.'

Mrs Clements agreed that mathematics would not clothe the babies, adding that she always tried to make her geography lessons relevant. No-one had ever complained about them before. Too prickly, thought Eileen. Mrs Clements, who was a capable teacher, saw all proposed changes as a personal criticism.

She supplied a suggested list of acquisitions for the library. An outraged Sister Jacinta refused to stock *The Second Sex* on her shelves.

'We must encourage all the girls to play sport, not just the keen ones. A healthy body comes from exercise. There's too much sitting around at lunchtime, too much gossiping, which leads to bitchiness and problems', she said another time. Mrs Clements later told Mrs Harvey that she was shocked at a nun saying 'bitchiness'. Mrs Harvey said they had to make allowances; Sister Eileen was still quite young and inexperienced. Things had been different in Mother Julian's time. I should jolly well think so, Eileen would have said had she heard the remark.

To set an example she coached the tennis team, Mrs McGee the basketball.

Pope John had exhorted them to be ecumenical, so they opened up the sports program to include competing against non-Catholic schools. Parents wondered if this were wise. To everyone's relief the moral tone of the school did not collapse, but the bishop became very concerned that the girls would meet non-Catholic boys. He didn't want too many mixed marriages in his diocese. It weakened the breeding strain.

By the end of the first year Eileen felt more confident. The external exam results were good. Next year, she decided, they would be excellent. Star of the Sea senior tennis team won the interschools championship.

Parents noted the external manifestations of success and were delighted. The older teachers worried about the relaxation of discipline and lack of respect. Girls looked like hoi polloi in their uniforms as hats and gloves became an anachronism. The teaching of Christian doctrine was getting out of hand. Class masses, with the girls crowded around the altar, not all looking reverent, caused distress. If Sister Rosaria had had to kneel at the altar rails, it didn't seem right that the whole of 10B, scalliwags most of them, should be allowed into the sanctuary. And prayers for the faithful which included petitions for sick budgerigars! There was a difference between informality and trivialising. Robbing the church of her ritual and ceremony was like dissipating the family inheritance. Once gone it was almost impossible to retrieve.

Eileen listened to the harbingers of doom. Then she listened to the younger, enthusiastic teachers, who warned her that if religion were not made meaningful to the young they would leave the church in droves. They needed to participate, feel part of God's loving family. That was the message of Vatican II. That was the message of John's gospel, very much in vogue.

Clare and Ted drove up, with their children, for her birthday, just before the end of the school year. A lovely day wandering about the countryside, finishing with a birthday tea at the local cafe. By that time Clare and Ted were well into parish reform. The obvious solution to all her problems was, they said, to hold a staff end-of-year mass. In the staff room, not the chapel.

Eileen cried herself to sleep the night after the staff mass, which had been the culmination of a tiring tension-filled week.

The omens had been good. Sister Regina had come across from the convent to join them. Sister Jacinta had helped prepare the staffroom, putting away the coffee cups, vacuum-cleaning the carpet, and placing a clean linen cloth on the low table. The art teacher had decorated two candles, and Mrs McGee had loaned a ceramic chalice and a plate for a paten. Father Stephen, a trendy from Clare's parish, had been happy to drive up to say their mass. Their parish priest, who tried to pretend Vatican II had never happened, had not been considered staff mass material.

So they sat on cushions on the floor, except for the Ancient Six: Sisters Jacinta, Theodore, Gerard, and Regina, Mrs Clements and Mrs Harvey, who sat on hard-backed chairs in a row at the end of the room. Spirals of incense smoke scented the stuffy room, making Sister Jacinta feel quite ill. Father Stephen, their celebrant, strode through the door. Mrs Harvey thought he looked like a pop singer, which was no compliment coming from her. When he boomed out: 'Well, let's get this show on the road', she closed her eyes in distress.

He began the mass with a hearty greeting, asked who had a birthday or anything special to celebrate, and who had special needs which they wanted to share with the others.

'I have a problem some of you know about already, but I'd like to share it with everyone', began Mrs Branigan. Miss Blackford frowned a signal which she ignored. 'My husband and I are having a few difficulties, lack of communication really, and the physical side of our relationship is not quite . . . quite, um, satisfactory. I think if we could get that together, then we could sort out the other areas of conflict. I'd like you to pray for us, please, in this mass.'

Mrs Clements was horrified. She'd picked up some of the story during recess and lunchtimes in the staffroom. But in front of Father Stephen! How could Jennifer say it? Luckily Sister Theodore was slightly deaf. Sister Jacinta surprised them all by muttering: 'Wrong way round. Conflicts sorted out, no worry about bedroom.'

Eileen thought that was what she said at the time, but later she wondered if she had imagined things, or simply heard her own thoughts being voiced in her head. She began to have serious doubts about Jennifer Branigan's discretion.

Miss Blackford confined herself to asking for prayers for a mother with suspected cancer, and Eileen, feeling that she had to show support, mentioned the school's continuing progress. Mrs Harvey and Mrs Clements said amen loudly to that one.

Those formalities over, Clare, who had driven up with Father Stephen to lend Eileen moral support and make sure all went as it should, strummed some chords on her guitar. She and Stephen began to sing a hymn which had featured in a popular musical. Clare said 'All together now' at the chorus. The younger teachers did their best; the Ancient Six sat in bewildered silence.

Stephen sang louder than anybody. It came as no surprise to Mrs Harvey later that he had defected from the priesthood and run away with one of his married parishioners. She could tell, even then.

The mass — if you could call it that, thought Sister Theodore — continued. They asked pardon for their sins in such a roundabout way that God probably didn't know what they wanted. Jennifer Branigan read from Kahlil Gihbran. Clare read from St Paul, very nicely, and the Ancient Six cheered up a little.

During the offertory Stephen invited them to kneel around the eucharistic table and hold hands. Eileen, Mrs Branigan, Mrs McGee, Miss Blackford, and Clare did as he asked. The others stayed where they were, hands firmly clasped in their laps. Not even during communion was there evidence of the cohesive Holy Spirit which Clare had promised her. The last hymn, 'I wanna be open to my Lord', sounded their knell.

They had tried. God knew they had entered that room in a spirit of Christian charity and openmindedness, but if Sister Eileen believed that this was the way to lead the school into modern church life, then God help her, the school, and the modern church. They could not believe that Pope John had meant the mass to be turned into a circus.

After the Six had retired, the others sat around on the floor and sang more hymns and protest songs while Clare accompanied them. Only Eileen, using work as her excuse, left. She just wanted to sit down quietly in her office and recover. It was all right for the others. They went home to husbands and families. She still had to face Sisters Jacinta, Theodore, Gerard, and Regina over the dinner table.

Actually things went a little better after that. Differences were polarised, acknowledged, and respected. Eileen knew that she could not push the older staff members too far. They were braked by too much old teaching. The younger teachers' revolutionary zeal was kept in check. The great star, Compromise, was in the ascendant.

Perhaps her greatest success story was Sister Theodore, who became the local expert on remedial maths, kept in constant demand as she went from problem school to conference. Sister Regina retired to the old convent, and Sister Gerard took over the housekeeping. Being of a less patient disposition than her predecessor, she organised a new stove within a matter of days.

After ten years the challenge had gone out of it. The country charm had palled. The girls had not become less bucolic. One of the fathers had created a minor distraction in her life, but that family had left the district. She was ready to move on, and had accepted the chance to be a parish worker with alacrity. Now that too had palled, but no, she did not want to go back to teaching.

Her thoughts were distracted by Clare and Lilian bringing her some travel brochures. Subtle pressure? They were due to leave for Europe in six weeks. Anne continued to write from Milan, where she was studying the influence of St Ambrose on St Augustine. Was there no end to the esoteric subjects on which to focus her academic zeal? Pauline was busy at the Caroline Chisolm Shelter, although she didn't always sleep there. She needed to get away, to draw breath. Eileen had privately thought that Pauline was not the right person to run a shelter for homeless girls, but she was being proved wrong. Pauline turned out to have the right mixture of realism and compassion.

Chapter Fifteen

All their bad news seemed to come by telephone. First it had been Mrs Cameron, then her father's stroke. So the telephone ringing at 11.30 in the evening evoked a warning response in Eileen's mind. Picking up the receiver hastily, she heard Karen's voice, raspy with anxiety. 'Have you seen Amber-Mae? She's run away.'

Eileen hadn't.

Karen told the story in incoherent bursts. Jimmy had come bursting in. He was very drunk, yelling and threatening. Amber-Mae had put on her dressing-gown and slippers and run out of the house while they were arguing. Jimmy stayed with Aaron while Karen walked the streets looking for her daughter. That was two hours ago. Her legs ached and she was worried. Had Amber-Mae gone to Eileen's?

No, she hadn't.

Eileen was dressed in a few minutes and out the door, pausing only to inform Pauline, standing at her bedroom door waiting to hear what the problem was. Incongruously Eileen noticed Pauline's face had Ponds vanishing cream, which hadn't totally vanished.

Through the night-deserted streets she walked, calling Amber-Mae's name softly, as though afraid to frighten the child by too much noise. Three blocks from her home she came to the park where she had sometimes taken Amber-Mae for a turn on the swings. The park was dark, spooky, threatening, but she did not hesitate, looking around the swings and slide, behind the sheltershed, and under the clump of bushes near the lake. Cowardice prevented her from looking too long at the murky water. If there were a small figure floating face downward, she didn't want to be the one to see it.

She sat on a park bench for a moment, trying to think where the little girl might have gone. Could she have been picked up by a stranger? There was always talk of a man hanging around the school. The lurking stranger had become as much a part of the neighbourhood as the local shop.

Her confused thoughts ranged between fear for Amber-Mae's safety, anger at Karen for taking so little care of her precious charge, and rage at Jimmy who had frightened her. If harm had come to the child, she felt she would not be able to bear it.

After an hour she returned home to ring Karen. Maybe there had been news.

The phone was answered by Jimmy, who told her curtly that Karen wasn't there then hung up. Not that Eileen wanted to exchange pleasantries.

Pauline, who had got up, insisted on her having a warm drink before she went out again. She drank it impatiently, tipping half down the sink so she could resume the search.

Stepping down the front steps she noticed a moving shadow near the front gate. Her heart leaped with hope. 'Amber-Mae?' she called.

Silence. Or did she hear a soft sound, more like a hiccup than a sob?

'Is that you, dear? Come over here.'

Was she being stupid, calling out to a phantom?

The shadow moved again. Karen called to her from the fence: 'It's only me. I came round to see if you had found her.'

'No', replied Eileen. 'I was just going out to have another look. Come inside for a moment.'

Instead, they sat on the front step.

Karen's face was streaked with tears; she walked with a limp due to a blistered heel.

'Exactly what happened?' Eileen asked her.

'I told you. Jimmy came in and Amber-Mae was frightened, so she snuck out. I'll kill her when I find her.'

'I thought Jimmy was in the country.'

'Nah. He came back soon after I did. He's been living with his brother's family. Sleeps in the back room. Doesn't like it, but. Reckons it's too far from the pub.'

'My heart bleeds for him', said Eileen sarcastically. 'So you hadn't seen him before tonight. Not since you left him, that is.'

'Sort of. He come around a couple of times, but only when the kids were asleep. I felt a bit sorry for him. He said he wanted us to get back together.'

'The fact that you live within walking distance of a pub had nothing to do with his desire for reconciliation, I presume', said Eileen, making no attempt to hide the disapproval in her voice.

'Hell, Sister. You're the nun, not me. I don't want to live on me own all me life. I like Jimmy when he's sober. He's a good bloke. Just gets silly when he's been drinking, that's all.'

'And had he been drinking tonight?'

'A bit.'

'Are you sure he didn't do something to upset Amber-Mae? It's not like her to run off for nothing.' Eileen's voice was sharper than she meant it to be.

'Doesn't matter what he did. My daughter's out there, lost. Could've been taken off by some pervert by now.'

As a diversionary tactic Karen's belligerence worked. Eileen got to her feet and said: 'You go to the left and I'll go right. Come back here in an hour if you haven't found her. Leave a message if you have.'

Eileen watched Karen walk down the road. Eileen could see the light of her torch waving about, getting smaller and fainter in the distance.

Relying on the streetlights and the moon, which appeared from time to time from behind a cloud, Eileen walked the opposite way to Karen. She thought of trying the school. Amber-Mae loved to watch the children playing at recess and lunchtime, while she talked about when she would go there.

Searching the playground revealed nothing. Eileen looked between the dark, shadowy classrooms. Surely she would have been too frightened to go there. Striding back towards the gate she saw something on the path. Bending down to look closer, she realised it was a child's slipper. Amber-Mae's? Karen had said she put on her dressing-gown and slippers before she went out. Poor little pet would have a sore, cold foot if she was wandering around with only one slipper.

Eileen called and called, as loudly as she could. Never mind the people sleeping in nearby houses. 'Amber-Mae, where are you? It's me, Sister Eileen. Amber-Mae!'

The distant sound of a car, an early rooster crowing from his backyard harem, dawn birds cheeping. No child replied.

Buoyed up by the clue of the slipper, she walked briskly around adjoining streets. Nothing. She went back to find Karen whitefaced with fatigue. She had had no success either.

'I'll go back home and see if she's there. If not, I'll ring the police.'

'Do you mean you haven't alerted them yet? They could have been out on patrol all night, looking for her. Sometimes you're very stupid Karen', snapped Eileen.

Karen's face crumpled.

'I know. I've made a mess of things. Jimmy said not to call them. He reckoned he'd get into trouble for hitting her.'

'But that was ages ago.'

'No. He hit her tonight as well. I didn't tell you before, because I knew you'd crack a fruity and blame me. I think he might've broke her arm. She ran off screaming. Jimmy tried to stop me following her, and by the time I got free of him she was gone.'

'In her slippers and dressing-gown?' asked Eileen, remembering the clue.

'Yes. I made her that dressing-gown', said Karen, now crying without control in the relief of revelation.

The front door opened. Pauline, awoken by the noise, came out to see if they had found Amber-Mae. Karen refused her offer of a warm drink and set off for her own home. Eileen also refused, saying she would have an hour's sleep now that Karen was going to ring the police. They could do the looking for a while.

Eileen slept until seven, waking with a start. There was a pain in her stomach as she remembered the events of the previous night. Slightly giddy from lack of sleep, she opened the front door to collect the morning paper. There, curled up on the mat, dirty and dishevelled, was Amber-Mae, fast asleep.

After the first rush of relief, Eileen was all cool efficiency, until, bending down to gently pick up the sleeping child, she saw the gash on her face, bruises around her eye, and her hand hanging at an awkward angle from her wrist. Then she felt sick with anger at the man who had abused this child.

'How could he do it? How could he be such a bully?' she said, more to herself than to Pauline, who had joined her.

'There's a lot of sick people in the world. I've learnt that in the short time I've been at the girls shelter. Bring her in and lie her on the couch. I'll get you a pillow and a blanket.'

Amber-Mae stirred slightly but did not wake up. They decided that the best thing was to take her straight to the hospital. Eileen carried her out to the car while Pauline rang Karen.

She arrived in record time at the hospital, where, as Sister Eileen, she visited the sick once a week, and, as the sister of Clare, she had called on a never-to-be-forgotten night. Now she was carrying Amber-Mae into casualty, holding her tightly to prevent her injured arm from moving unnecessarily.

The intern, having had a quiet night, was delighted to finish his shift dealing with a patient. He made no comment about her battered face but moved her injured arm very gently and decided it would have to be X-rayed. Amber-Mae, now awake, was clinging to Eileen as the only familiar figure in this maze of alienation.

A distraught Karen ran to meet them as they returned from casualty. 'Gawd, look at her face. The mongrel! Come here. Come to Mummy.'

Amber-Mae, lying on a trolley, groggy from a sedative, clung to Eileen's hand.

'I think she's still confused. The doctor said her wrist is broken. He's put it in plaster', said Eileen.

'Give her here', said Karen, holding out her arms to take her daughter. 'Jimmy's outside in the car. He can drive us home.'

Eileen froze. No way was she sending Amber-Mae back with that monster. 'The doctor says she needs to sleep. Let me take her to my place, where she can sleep in peace and quiet. That will give you time to sort out everything with Jimmy. I can't imagine why you wanted to see him again after this business', said Eileen.

Clare would have laughed at her naivety.

It might have turned into a tug of war if the doctor hadn't intervened, saying he would only allow Amber-Mae out of the hospital if she went home with Eileen. Karen agreed to the arrangement. She sensed continued protest would not further her cause.

'You lot stick together, don't you?' was her parting shot as she limped down the hospital corridor.

Chapter Sixteen

Amber-Mae slept most of the first day in the couch-bed made up in the spare room. Occasionally she cried out in her sleep, and Eileen would rush in to soothe and comfort. Her broken wrist did not seem to give her too much discomfort and the marks on her face began to heal.

Karen was still sorting things out with Jimmy, who was anxious to have a united family that included his son but not his stepdaughter.

Although the doctor had made little comment on Amber-Mae's injuries, he knew enough of the story to decide he should report Amber-Mae as an abused child. This led to Welfare 'poking their noses in where they're not wanted', as Karen put it to Eileen. Would Eileen be an angel and have Amber-Mae with her for a bit longer? Eileen was happy to agree.

For the next few days she was mother. She remembered to cancel some of her meetings, just not turning up for the others. Amber-Mae took up all her time and attention.

They went to the zoo the first day. Amber-Mae threw back her head and laughed with glee at the antics of the baby giraffe. The orang-outang frightened her, gibbering at her through the bars of his enclosure. It took an ice-cream and a most unhealthy looking bun to settle her nerves so that she could really appreciate the baby animals in the zoo nursery.

That evening things were tense at the community house. Pauline had returned for a 'few hours peace and quiet'. Amber-Mae, querulous with fatigue, threw her bread and honey on the floor and cried for her mother. Eileen wasn't feeling a ball of energy either. She would have liked to join Pauline in a quiet cup of tea. Amber-Mae did settle after a warm bath and a story and several drinks of water, and another story, and having the light on, then off, then on, then a piece of bread and honey. Finally, silence.

'One can almost sympathise with Jimmy', said Pauline, but Eileen was in no mood to joke about it.

Clare, who had been kept abreast by her social worker friend ('Strictly Confidential' had its limits), called to see how she was coping with her young visitor.

'Now you're finding out how the other half lives', she said. 'Welfare are unhappy about the child going back to the mother while she is with her de facto. Karen is unhappy about giving up Jimmy. Jimmy is unhappy about being father to the child of a man he hates. The whole thing's a mess.'

'Why doesn't Karen just choof Jimmy off and settle down to being a mother to her two children? The solution is obvious', replied Eileen.

'It's more complex than that', said Clare, trying to explain. 'Maybe, in the shelter of your convent, you have not noticed, but people are very intricate beings.'

Eileen hated it when Clare referred to 'the shelter of your convent'. She felt that she dealt with life in all its reality and that her perspectives were sharper because she had a spiritual dimension. It was like being part of something yet separate.

The following day she went to visit her parents, taking Amber-Mae with her. Eileen's mother took Amber-Mae to the kitchen for the regulation drink and biscuit. Eileen sat on the front verandah, talking to her father. She told him that while she had the child to worry about she couldn't consider going overseas.

There was a wad of messages waiting for her when she returned. Pauline was slumped in a chair, saying she had had a cow of a day and was absolutely exhausted. 'You have no idea how awful those girls can be. They would try the patience of a saint, and, Lord knows, I'm no saint', she moaned.

Amber-Mae, grizzly with fatigue, needed to be bathed, fed, read to, prayed with, settled into bed, and comforted until she finally went to sleep.

Eileen slumped into the chair opposite Pauline and asked: 'Whose turn is it to cook dinner?'

'Turn? We gave up turns weeks ago. Whoever has the energy. I think I'd rather fast than make the effort to cook', said Pauline with a yawn.

They settled for tinned tomatoes on toast.

On the third day Amber-Mae was fractious indeed. Her arm itched under the plaster but she screamed when Eileen tried to scratch it with a knitting needle. After breakfast she settled down to playing with blocks while Eileen finally found time to sort out and deal with her messages. They had a lovely busy morning together, driving to the shops, stopping at the swings on the way back, then watching children's television. Eileen had learnt her lesson from the previous two days and put Amber-Mae down for a sleep in the afternoon. In the quiet house she sat reading her Bible, feeling satisfied that she had done something specific to help another human person.

When you were hungry I gave you something to eat . . . when

you were tired I gave you a place to rest, she thought to herself. Pauline didn't come home that night, so she couldn't go to the catechists meeting because she couldn't leave the child on her own. She knew that the catechists would cope very well without her.

The blow fell on the fourth day. Karen had agreed to allow Amber-Mae to go into foster care. She was going back up the country with Jimmy and Aaron. Clare rang to tell Eileen that the Welfare people would come around the next day to collect Amber-Mae. The child would be protected from abuse and would be well looked after by her foster parents. It wasn't the perfect solution, but there you are.

'There you are, where?' answered Eileen, in shock. 'Why can't she stay with me instead of going to strangers? We're getting on just fine.'

'I thought you'd be glad to get rid of her. It can't be easy for you to have her staying there. We think you've been an angel.'

That word again! She was not an angel but a flesh-and-blood woman.

'Tomorrow won't be convenient. Tell Welfare, or whoever, that Amber-Mae is staying with me until I am satisfied she's going to a better home than the one I can give her. I have invested a lot of time in the child.' She added the last sentence, a term she had heard Clare use many times, to add weight to her words. Before Clare had time to reply she added a polite goodbye and hung up.

Her knees were trembling so much she had to sit down on the nearest chair. She had known that they would take the child away from her, but not yet. Not until she had prepared herself.

'I joined a community of over one hundred nuns, and now, twenty-five years later, I am in a community of one and a half. Amber-Mae being here makes it two and a half.' Eileen was talking to herself, thinking out loud.

Amber-Mae, having heard the phone and then voices, came running out of her bedroom. 'Is Mummy here?' she asked, face alight.

Before Eileen could answer she went into the kitchen, returning a few seconds later with tears welling in her eyes.

'Where's my mummy? Can I go home? I want to go home.'

'Of course you do', Eileen said, and meant it. 'Come and sit on my knee for a bit till you feel better.'

Amber-Mae climbed up and nestled comfortably until she fell asleep. Eileen carried her carefully to her bed and tucked her in.

A knock at the door. So late? More trouble?

It was Clare, red hair in a frenzy. 'What is all this nonsense about letting Welfare know when you are ready? You have no rights over this child. Wake up to yourself, Eileen. Don't let your do-gooding get out of hand.'

Eileen hit back. 'Do you know a better way? You killed your last baby. If you didn't want it I would have brought it up. With love and caring.'

Now that it was said they both felt better. Clare's tone softened. 'If you want a child you can have your own. It's not too late. There are hundreds of single mothers.'

'Don't mock me', replied Eileen. 'I expected more from you.'

'No I'm not. Just take stock for a moment. You have choices. You don't have to stay trapped. There's a whole world out there waiting for you if you only have the courage to break free and become part of it.'

There it was again. The assumption that she was not part of the real world. Was that how Karen saw her? And Amber-Mae?

They sat in silence for a while, each engrossed in her thoughts. Clare could understand Eileen's desire for a child. Eileen could never explain to Clare that her need to stay faithful to her vocation was greater still than any desire for human fulfilment.

'I'm sorry I said that about killing your baby. It was a nasty and uncalled-for comment', Eileen finally said, breaking the silence.

'I'm sorry that I didn't really understand how attached you were to Amber-Mae. I should have realised. Why don't you pray about it?' replied Clare.

'I do, but I don't feel that anybody is listening.'

No more was said on the subject. The time for complete honesty and self-revelation had passed.

Chapter Seventeen

Clare finalised the arrangements for Amber-Mae to be collected. Karen had already gone to the country. She didn't think she could face saying goodbye to her daughter. She would wait until Amber-Mae was settled in and then call and see her. Welfare had thought this was a good idea.

After Clare left, Eileen went to her room. Prayer, she thought — that is the answer. Pray for guidance and wisdom. Jesus, she knew, had often prayed throughout the night. She had never felt she had the stamina. But this night she fell on her knees and wrestled with her soul till dawn. This night she prayed with such intensity that she knew Someone was listening.

Eileen knew she had choices. She didn't need Clare to tell her that. She could leave the order, as had Anne, take time off and travel. Maybe get married and have a child. It was still biologically possible. She could stay as she was — Sister Eileen, parish worker. She could ask the order to find her different work. The vineyard was not overstocked with labourers.

'Seek ye first the kingdom of God.' That kingdom was within.

'Be still, and listen.' When had she had time to be still and listen? When, lately, had she made time?

'The peace of God surpasseth all understanding.' She hungered for that peace.

The next day she packed up Amber-Mae's few possessions and told her that she was going for a short holiday with a nice family, who had a dog and a cat, and she would see her mummy a bit later.

The welfare officer came straight after lunch. Amber-Mae clung to Eileen's hand at first, then, after some coaxing, went off with a cheery wave and a smile. Eileen would keep the memory of the golden-haired cherub waving through the car window. She wondered what life held in store for Amber-Mae.

Clare rang her that night to see how she was taking it. 'Now you can come overseas after all. Dad told me you said you couldn't because of the child. Why not leave at the same time as Lilian and I?'

But Eileen knew what she was going to do. She packed her clothes, then sat down to write a long letter to Mother Provincial and a note for Pauline. She had already informed Father Tom.

As the train rumbled through the countryside Eileen closed her eyes with weariness. In an hour she would be at her destination.

In her letter to the provincial she had tried to explain that she needed time to be spiritually replenished. The Carmelites had agreed to her staying with them for a month, two months, or even three, depending on how long she needed. She would spend the time in almost total silence, prayer, and meditation, living and working with the Carmelite nuns.

Sister Josephine had said a vocation was a call from God. She had answered that call as a very young girl. God was calling her again, but to what? In the silence and peace of Carmel she would discover it, and she would pray that she had the courage to say: 'Thy will be done'.